LOKUM

LOKUM

SELİN KAHRAMANOĞLU

Publisher and acquiring editor: Meghan Macdonald | Editor: Andrea Wilmot
Cover design and illustration: Laura Boyle

Library and Archives Canada Cataloguing in Publication

Title: Lokum / Selin Kahramanoğlu.
Names: Kahramanoğlu, Selin, author.
Identifiers: Canadiana (print) 20250310821 | Canadiana (ebook) 20250315416 | ISBN 9781459757004 (softcover) | ISBN 9781459757028 (EPUB) | ISBN 9781459757011 (PDF)
Subjects: LCGFT: Novels.
Classification: LCC PS8621.A45 L65 2026 | DDC C813/.6—dc23

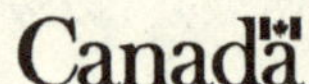

We acknowledge the support of the Canada Council for the Arts and the Ontario Arts Council for our publishing program. We also acknowledge the financial support of the Government of Ontario, through the Ontario Book Publishing Tax Credit and Ontario Creates, and the Government of Canada.

Printed and bound in Canada.

Rare Machines, an imprint of Dundurn Press
1382 Queen Street East
Toronto, Ontario, Canada M4L 1C9
dundurn.com, @dundurnpress

Ablama
and to the storytellers

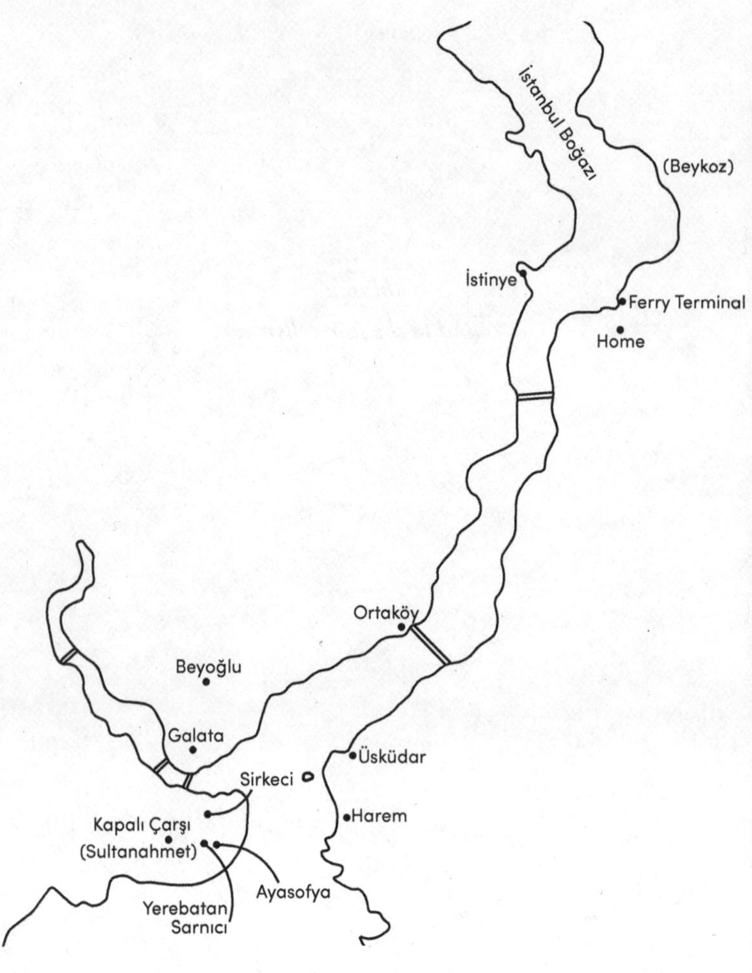
İstanbul Boğazı
(Beykoz)
İstinye
Ferry Terminal
Home
Ortaköy
Beyoğlu
Galata
Üsküdar
Sirkeci
Harem
Kapalı Çarşı
(Sultanahmet)
Ayasofya
Yerebatan
Sarnıcı

LOKUM

Pronounced lo-*koom*: Turkish delight — a small, chewy candy made of cornstarch, lemon juice, and sugar, with additional flavourings. It is usually sweet and bite-sized and is often served alongside bitter Turkish coffee.

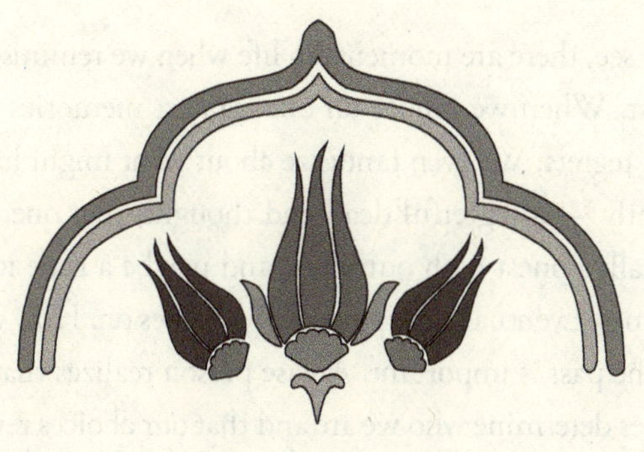

PROLOGUE

I have a request.

I know, I know, we are practically strangers — I am so sorry to disrupt your peace, by the way. Asking you for a favour does not offer a very good first impression of me; I am aware of it. But please, hear me out. I think this little request might benefit you, too. If you could trust me just this once, you might come to thank me one day.

Of course, I'll explain everything. You can decide for yourself if you are willing to help me. Though, before I ask something of you, I should probably tell you one thing. If you would indulge me, I'm going to get a little sentimental.

You see, there are moments in life when we reminisce about our past. When we reflect on our fondest memories and our deepest regrets. We even fantasize about what might have gone differently — a regretful dead-end thought, that one. We can be brutally honest with ourselves, and maybe a little too harsh sometimes. Eventually, we learn that life goes on. How we think about the past is important. A wise person realizes that our experiences determine who we are and that our choices reveal who we wish to be. We understand that when we accept our past, we unlock our potential. We grow and become better people.

You are still following me, yes?

Some of us, however, deny our past and hide it away. We lie to ourselves, thinking that our histories don't matter. Undoubtedly, they *do* matter. We shouldn't forget what has happened to us — the people we've met who have shaped us into who we are today. We cannot appreciate the sweetness in life without experiencing its bitterness, too.

Okay then, back to the matter at hand. Like I said, I need your help. What I'm asking is very simple. You see, I would like to share a memory, one that is threatening to fade into the recesses of my mind. I'm sure that once I've told you what it is, you will understand why it is important to relive it. I am starting to forget it already. With each passing day, this memory fades a little more. I want to share it with someone before it disappears forever. I hope that by relaying it to you, the memory, my story will survive a few generations more.

The story can help you, too. Not just *you* specifically, of course, because I don't know you very well, but anyone who hears it. I promise you it truly is a wondrous story that sparkles in the mind. Like a star that has guided me my entire life, I want to relay it to you in hopes that your gaze will keep it aglow.

As you read these words, let my thoughts become yours. Borrow my eyes, my ears, my heart. I hope that by showing you what I love, you will come to love it, too. Learn from my mistakes. Take my lessons with you. Live through my memory — try to understand why I acted as I did.

This story is both an invitation and a weapon for those who know how to listen.

You're still here, so I assume you've accepted my hand and are ready to leave harbour together. We're headed to an extraordinary corner of the world, and I will share with you every sound, smell, and colour we encounter. We travel to a city that is the product of both Europe and Asia, an ancient host for peoples all over the world and a perfect spot for storytelling. Full of legends, full of lessons. My friend, I welcome you to İstanbul.

• • •

You see, I grew up a citizen of two countries. My Turkish parents immigrated to Canada days after they married, taking a risk by choosing to start the next phase of their life there. My sister and I were born near Toronto, but we spoke only Turkish in our early years. We both still live in Canada, and we have a deep appreciation for being on these lands. Do not think of us as only Canadians, though, because that would be false. Growing up, we never felt deprived of our Turkish heritage. We were always surrounded by immigrant Turks and friends from other cultures. We have a good life in Canada and have maintained a strong connection to our family's culture. A common story for many immigrants.

As a child, many of my summer months were spent in İstanbul. We visited every year, catching up with family and friends. As I grew older, I established a few preferred spots in the city and even adopted local slang and mannerisms. My family travelled to different parts of Türkiye to explore and learn more about our history. Türkiye is where I find my ancestors, the origins of my customs and values, my connection to community. In Türkiye, my roots run deep, and if I stay away for too long, my heart seems to grow weaker. With all its highs and lows, I always feel like I have a home there.

So you see, I did not grow up with only one language or country. Proudly, I am a citizen of two nations equally. Being a child of immigrants, we know of empathy, overcoming hardship, and evolving in response to the environment around us. To others, this may be difficult to understand, but my identity can be explained very simply: Canada serves as my brain — my rational thinking, my views of the world, and my criticisms. Türkiye is my heart — my passions, my understandings of loss and love, the strength of my intuition and soul. I do not adore one identity more than the other, nor can one country replace the other. I need both. I *am* both.

Why am I telling you this? For this memory to make sense, you need to know that this duality exists within me at all times. It is thanks to this blessing that I see the world a little differently. I embody two different lifestyles, two mentalities, two lenses through which to view the world. This story that I am about to share with you is an example of this very duality. This memory, this story, was developed at the intersection of these two cultures, which coexist within me, for better or for worse.

Now you may dive into my memory fully prepared for the experience. I'm going to tell you the story now, yes? You are comfortable and have a little snack next to you? Perfect. I sincerely hope that it is worth the journey. Make good use of this memory. Remember, no need to panic if you get lost. And as my grandmother would say, don't forget to drink water.

Yolunuz açık olsun.*

---

* For translations and explanations of Turkish words, expressions, and gestures, refer to the glossary on page 203.

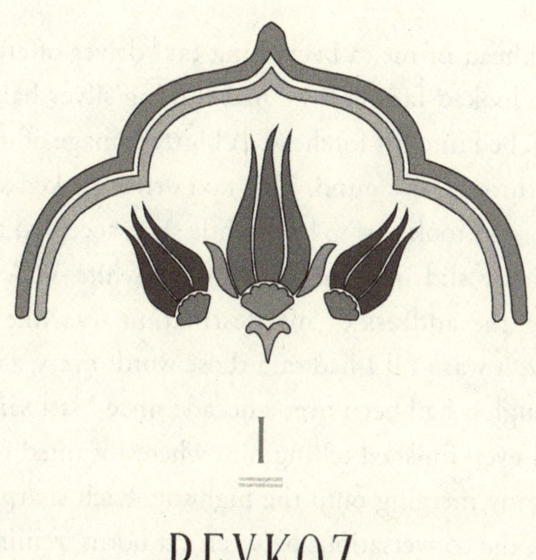

I

BEYKOZ

Thankfully, it seems I hadn't completely forgotten everything.

After fifteen years away, there are still some things about İstanbul that stick in my mind, like the honey left behind on my fingertips after eating a date. Stepping out of Atatürk Airport in the late afternoon, among sweet wisps of cigarette smoke, I was met with the ever-present crowd outside the international arrivals terminal. As soon as I exited the building, the fragrant heat of the air jolted awake my memories of Türkiye, which had long been asleep.

Just ahead of me, a beckoning taxi driver offered me a ride. He looked familiar; he had shining silver hair, wrinkles sketched into his forehead. A blurred image of my uncle flashed through my mind. This taxi driver looked so much like him — I took this to be a gentle sign, accepted the ride, and quickly slid into the back of the white Volkswagen. Reciting the address of my destination was like muscle memory; it was as if I had said those words every day of my life, though it had been over a decade since I last said them. Before I even finished telling him where I wanted to go, he was already merging onto the highway. Each sharp turn of the taxi, the conversations between car horns, reminded me of İstanbul's constant traffic. I was so busy trying to process the sudden rush of memories that I hadn't realized how quickly we were moving. Before I knew it, we were approaching the exit for the bridge.

"You seem tired. Heading home?" asked the driver, glancing at me in the rearview mirror with his light blue eyes. I suppose I had bags under mine, thanks to two days of travelling.

"Yes, but only for a little while," I replied honestly.

"Hoş geldiniz. Were you away long, my friend?"

These drivers were always so perceptive. I thought of them as the faithful veins that carry people around this heart of a city. I noticed his nametag on the visor — Asaf.

"It doesn't feel that way," I told him.

"Ah, I understand. İstanbul never leaves *us*, even when we leave *it*."

I nodded. "You couldn't be more right."

I opened the window an inch with the handle crank, and the scent of ripened oregano and blossoming linden trees invaded the car. This fading dream of İstanbul had rapidly become intensely real, and that well-known warmth returned to my skin. I watched the passing towns as they blended together: pastel-coloured houses of yellow, pink, green, blue, all of them a hazy palette spread out across the horizon, with trees of different kinds competing for the spaces between the structures.

Suddenly, from several hilltops all at once, minarets mimicked one another as an echoing azan struck my ears. The call to prayer rose up, becoming part of the breeze, synchronizing with the quieting of car radios along the road. I was entranced by the melodic lyrics, the spice in the air, and the familiarity of it all. It was nearly five in the evening. As I noticed the sun's rays beaming into the car, warming my arm and bleaching the hairs there, I remembered the symptoms of summertime in this country. Before I arrived, I was beginning to think that these experiences weren't real, that I had only imagined these characteristics of İstanbul. Though many years had passed, I was relieved to find that this place was not a fantasy. It was as if my ongoing lie was miraculously truthful. Entirely at ease, I closed my eyes to the hum of the azan.

"Hmm, so you were away a long time," the driver said, interrupting my thoughts. "What brings you back to the city?"

I have always thought that taxi drivers can be a little too curious about the lives of their passengers.

"My sister's getting married," I answered.

"Ah, congratulations. May Allah give her a healthy family and patience with her husband." Asaf's eyes crinkled at his own joke.

I faked a laugh. "Thank you, I hope so."

If it weren't for my sister's marriage, I might never have returned to this place. I could argue that life became busier once I finished school and started working, or that money was scarce and I wasn't able to pay for the flight, but neither of these reasons was accurate. Really, I thought I didn't need to come back. The remainder of my family had either died, moved to other cities, or immigrated to Canada with us. Our childhood house in the Beykoz district became a summer house. No one except my aunt returned to that place, and even she only stayed a couple of months throughout the whole year.

There was no reason for me to come back to this city. My family was no longer here. My job was elsewhere. My home, my friends, my hobbies were all rooted in Canada.

I have returned to this place by force. Nergiz, my sister, is a fan of nostalgia. She's getting married in the same historical building that my parents did. The wedding is being held in our old neighbourhood so that the senior generations of her many guests can attend and so that we can use the summer house for preparations. The event is the day after tomorrow, but I have arrived early to become reacquainted with the city. I am curious to see which things have changed and how unreliable my memories have become these past few years.

I can't complain, having been lucky enough to experience a wonderful life in Canada. I've had a great education, which took up most of my youth. I have dependable friends, a caring family, and an enjoyable job. As a community outreach librarian, I develop programs and educational tools to help orient children and young newcomers in their new Canadian lives, showing them how they can stay in touch with their own unique cultural identities. I show them what is familiar and comforting, but also what is full of opportunity. I grew up figuring it out by myself and have learned a few tricks to share. I've found more Turks and other immigrants of similar backgrounds to my own. They've shared their stories with me, helped keep my culture alive. Still, despite these privileges, it has become clear to me that something is still missing from my life. A dullness that has built over time, muting all of life's colours with every year that I grow older. I feel like I have been distanced from something real. I am certain that a tangible and fulfilling life was once in my possession, but it has since faded. I held it in my hands once, a long time ago, but I do not know where it went or why it has left me. I wonder if I somehow deserved to lose it, not knowing something was good until it was gone. Some of my friends have speculated it was homesickness or depression creeping in; possibly both. My life has been rather routine, and no matter what I've tried, I have lived my days like a passenger. Flatlined rather than upbeat, my heart is now existing in a prison that I created for myself.

It is true that with each passing year, we returned to Türkiye less frequently. Now, it's been fifteen years since my last trip here. And while I've come back for my sister's wedding, I have this feeling that there is more to do here. There is something in this city that I need, but I do not understand what form that need will take. This void in my soul has grown with each year of my life, and I am desperate to know the reason. Why here? Why is it that the moment I arrived at the airport, I felt as if I was healing an old wound? Why is İstanbul so important to me? All I know is that my heart hurts; it sinks deeper into my chest, compact and heavy, and my mind is at a loss as to what to do about it.

As the azan ended, the driver turned the radio back up.

"You should go to the beach after the wedding," Asaf remarked. "You're pale, my friend. Is there no sun where you were staying? You look like a foreigner."

His comment seemed like another joke at first, but there was real concern in his words.

I gave a small smile and assured him, "There is sun there, but longer winters. Hopefully I'll get to take your advice and find a beach sometime soon."

The driver changed gears and reached for his ringing phone with the other hand. He guided the steering wheel with his knees.

"I know a good place, if you need recommendations," he said. Asaf picked up the phone but didn't speak into it right away. "My brother runs a little pide stall near Şile. It's not too far from you, I think. The beaches around his stall are nice. You can get a good tan there."

I smiled at his sincerity. "I will be sure to look for it."

Smelling the fresh herbs wafting in through the open window, memories at the back of my mind kept being triggered. Before coming to the city, I had been afraid that I had completely forgotten İstanbul. Childhood photo albums can remind us of only so much. This visit might help return some vibrant colour to those faded photographs. We had only been driving for an hour or so, but already, breathing this air, I felt hope fill my chest.

Life has brought me back here. I have a feeling this trip might save me.

Please do not mistake me; I do not mean to complain. My life is full of good fortune, and I am not ungrateful. I am not without a home or people who love me. I am safe. I am very appreciative of all the little moments that have enriched my life;

however, if I could be permitted this one selfishness, I would like to ask for something more. You could say that I'm lacking … flavour? Honestly, my life in Canada is a little mild. There is no sparkle, no mystery, not even some drama in my life. Things have started to look dull, and I lack motivation to pursue the many adventures that life has to offer. Someone as young as me should have an appetite for the wild, the passionate side of life, yet I do not. My eyes see this world in monochrome, and it's slowly killing me. Stability is my problem, I think. It's so predictable. So, I've come to İstanbul. There is activity here. Hopefully, by being back in the space that once inspired such treasured memories, I will fall in love with life once again.

The taxi rolled to a stop as we approached the end of the bridge. The driver told the caller on the phone to hold on a minute. Asaf addressed me through the rearview mirror.

"Sorry, my friend," he said, sounding irritated. "You know, this is the worst time of day to cross the Bosphorus, this traffic will make you late for tea every time." He sighed loudly and added, "These idiots won't budge for a while. You'll have to be a little more patient to get home."

Hanging my hand out the window's edge, slouching into the bead-covered backseat, I kept my eyes fixed on the ferries streaking the turquoise coast below. A smile was pulling at the corners of my mouth once again.

"Don't worry about it," I assured him. "I can wait a little more."

When the road cleared up, my driver quickly finished his phone call and indulged me with an update on the growth of İstanbul. We talked for the remainder of the ride, and when we finally reached the old house, I knew of all the latest events.

It was true that the simit vendors still roamed the streets, and fisherman continued to line the Bosphorus shoreline. Meanwhile, traffic jams did not cease to exist in the earliest hours of the morning, even though the ferries that operated every half hour were packed with crowds. Citizens were still arguing over which government should be in power, though everyone agreed that politics were not progressing at all. Each town's weekly pazar still kept farmers in business, but the banks were just as frustrating as ever. My taxi driver was especially tired of there being too many people in the city, locals and foreigners alike, but all of this was not new. The names of some parks and streets were different now, and bus fares had changed, but these were all surface-level details. Essentially, nothing much was different — İstanbul was as it always had been. This made me a little happier.

Incredibly, my mind had maintained a true likeness of my beloved city. I stopped coming back to Türkiye at the age of eighteen, but I never abandoned my culture when I decided to stay in Canada. I know how to make Turkish foods and when to celebrate bayram. I can direct people to the best cafes in the Taksim district, like I do for my tourist friends that visit İstanbul. I know about all the traditions of Ramazan and wedding ceremonies. Still, I can't brag too much, because everything I remember about İstanbul is a reiteration of stories that I've been told, photos that I've seen, or memories from years ago, all of which are not very reliable anymore. I'm sure more things have changed. I have certainly changed.

Why do my eyes sting with tears when I have to leave this city? I don't know. I *do* know that these forgotten memories are the reasons why İstanbul continues to have a hold over me. Who was I before I left here? Why was I so happy here, and where did all of those good feelings go? I suppose this is what people might call an existential crisis.

This trip needed to be made, with or without Nergiz's wedding. All it took was a few hours under the Near Eastern sun and a spark was lit inside my heart. I'm tired of this flavourless, average world that I have built for myself. Tomorrow, I will explore the city and reintroduce its spices to my life. No more delays. This journey begins now.

• • •

The old house looked the same. The gate opened with a short squeak, revealing a familiar 150-year-old building. Our home's pastel yellow walls peeked out from behind the thick leaves of the unripe erik and fig trees that lined the gate. Blossoming roses met my feet as I reached the bottom of the wood staircase.

The soil was dewed with yesterday's rain; tomato and cucumber vines intertwined in the vegetable garden. The storage shed didn't look any rustier than it had the last time I'd seen it, but the locks appeared new. The clotheslines that were strung between the house and the shed were bare, dangling above cement floors. Turning the corner, the scent of white jasmine filled my nose as grapevines gently swept the top of my hair. Moving through the garden, my feet tried to dodge decades of fallen mulberries that stained the ground with blemishes of mauve. The wind was stronger on our hillside and would occasionally gust, causing the leaves to roar and drowning out the sounds of chickens from the neighbouring yards.

"Thank you," I whispered to the air. My aunt was taking good care of this place.

I searched my duffle bag for a frail key and was surprised to be able to open the door without any struggle. For such an old house, the air inside was still — I didn't feel a single draft dancing through the halls. The floor was not cold; rather, an elaborate rug hugged my tired feet. I plopped myself down on one of the couches. They were hard but springy, and I sat down on the same cushion that I'd sat on as a two-year-old. The faintest layer of dust ghosted the top of framed pictures, while porcelain figurines of whirling dervishes and fancy dishware sat undisturbed in the glass cabinet. It was as if nothing had been touched in all the time I'd been away — as if I was last here only days ago and not fifteen years.

I didn't feel alone, sitting there in the silence of the empty house. Having been gone for many years, I expected to feel like an invader within these walls, but instead I felt right at home. Everything was exactly how we'd left it. It was almost seven o'clock now, and I could practically smell my aunt grilling the köfte in the kitchen while my mother chopped fresh mint for the çoban salad. I could almost hear my other aunt calling for my sister and me to set the table for ten people. I could picture my cousin opening the window to call my uncle, father, and grandfather to come inside from the shed. All of this while imagining my grandmother searching the hallway cabinets for her best tablecloth. I could see it all, unfolding in front of my eyes as I sat there in the stillness. Dusk descended upon İstanbul's Beykoz district.

Normally, when I am deep in thought, I jump at a phone ringing suddenly. This time, however, the sound was so in character, so timed to my memory, that I almost didn't realize it was actually ringing. How realistic, to have someone calling our house just as we were about to sit at my imaginary dinner table. I reached for the phone.

"Buyrun?" I croaked.

"Kuzum, have you arrived?" asked my aunt. She'd spoken loudly, though I'm sure she meant to be gentle. She didn't wait for my answer. "I thought that you would call me when you arrived? Did you have a good flight? Have you eaten? Aren't you excited for your sister's wedding? What a blessing this is! Thankfully, all the preparations are complete. May Allah finally give us all peace and rest when it is over. There was so much to do. So many people are coming! Yavrum, are you there?"

"Yes —"

"ALO?" she shouted.

"YES," I shouted back. "I'm here! Thank you for all your help with the wedding. You can rest easy."

"Of course!" She spoke with bounce in her voice. "May Allah give you your own wedding someday. You should sleep early tonight, and I will see you at dinner tomorrow evening to talk final plans before the big day! Are you sure you don't want me to take you to breakfast tomorrow? My eyebrow appointment isn't until noon, then my nails, which probably won't take too long ..."

"No, no, I wanted to explore the city a little," I interjected. "Thanks for the offer. Let me know if you need me to bring anything to dinner at the last minute. Tamam?"

"Tamam, kuzum. Görüşürüz," she said, her voice fading. She hung up.

I dragged my luggage up the spiral stairs and into my old bedroom. It was my father's room first, and it still had all his engineering textbooks in it. There were even shelves of books from his time in high school, crammed with mostly English classical literature. Only the bedsheets were mine, and they still had the same fading striped pattern from when I was a child. The air was warmer and stuffier upstairs, and I wrestled with the sticky window handle to let the freshness in. As soon as I managed to open it and the breeze hit my face, the annoying sound of a buzzing mosquito attacked my ears. Some things never change.

Making my way back downstairs, I headed to my favourite spot on the property. The balcony was wide and sparse, with only a dining table and plastic chairs tucked into its corner. The tiles had a light pink cloud design, and the white-painted stone balcony wall came up to my mid-thigh. Even in the descending night sky, the houses below kept the same colourful hues. In the distance, the clatter of plates and laughter could be heard from the closest café. My eyes settled on the horizon, the ships there drifting on the Bosphorus, barely visible except for their guiding lights.

I thought about what I wanted to do. After the wedding, our family would no doubt be jumping between visits with the extended family. If I wanted to explore İstanbul on my own, I'd have to do it tomorrow, before the dinner party. But where should I go? Which places were most important to me? Could I even see everything in a day? It was impossible. There was so much crammed into this city. I needed to pick my highlights. What if one of my favourite places had been torn down at some point during the last decade? I didn't have any answers and could not consider that right then. There was much to do and I had only one day.

Wafting saltwater filled my nose, and a cool wind shook my brain awake, sent a shiver down my spine. I knew where to go. I didn't plan out the whole day, but the route was slowly taking shape in my mind. I was confident that I would get to see all my favourite places and still make it in time for the pre-wedding family dinner.

Breathing in the air of the nearby Bosphorus, I felt cleansed. Despite my weariness, my spirit felt light. I was hopeful that my day trip would bring rejuvenation. I was excited to see what magic İstanbul had in store for me, and I knew exactly where to start. I needed to be by the water.

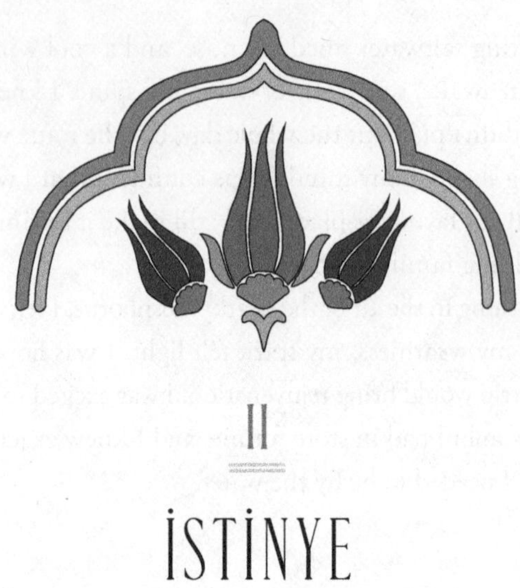

II

İSTİNYE

I was a little out of practice when it came to travelling longer distances, so I fell asleep as soon as my head hit the pillow. Nevertheless, my excitement about returning to the city didn't allow me to sleep in for very long. I awoke to the sounds of the morning azan and was pleased to be greeted with a gentle yellow-green glow of daylight on the horizon.

After a brief time wrestling with the water heater, I showered greedily, causing steam to seep out under the bathroom door. There were no groceries in the house, so I grabbed a barely ripened fig from the tree in the garden and gently rubbed it between my palms before taking a bite. It oozed sweet nectar, which dripped down the corners of my mouth. I recalled an image — my sister at probably seven years old, buried beneath the huge leaves of the tree. My father was instructing her on how to tell which figs were ripe. She was filling a bowl that I was holding, and I had fig honey in my hair, making it sticky. I heard him say "Aferin" as she reached for another fig, and the memory faded.

I took another fruit from the tree and then left the garden, using the stone staircase nearby as a shortcut straight down the hillside. Bending my head under the overgrown linden trees, I made my way to the main street below. Once there, my eyes started darting around as I took in the stillness of the neighbourhood, the houses cracking at their foundations from their mature age. A breeze tickled my nose as I breathed in a confusing mixture of dust and lemon scent. The small businesses along the road had changed, but the old bakery was still there. Peering in, I saw dim lights inside, but it was too early and they weren't open yet. There was a stray black Labrador sleeping among the weeds along the side wall, and I caught the smell of fresh bread escaping the window above him. I continued along my path, passing a small playground set between two convenience stores. There was rusty exercise equipment near the swings, which looked as worn down as the rest of Beykoz. I had just begun to wonder if our neighbourhood had always looked this tired when a garish ferry boat horn almost made me jump out of my shoes.

"Korkma, şekerim," a small beggar woman said quietly as she cradled a toddler. Her clothes were torn and covered in dirt. "The first ferry of the day has arrived at the port." She spoke in a raspy northeastern dialect. "You have woken up quite early to catch it. I would hurry. Oh, and next week, they will change the ferry times again, in case you didn't know."

Her eyes were sunken, surrounded by dark circles. I extended my second fig to the child in her arms, who immediately grabbed it but did not eat it.

"Eat, my son," she said gently. "It will taste sweeter, since it came from this kind traveller's hands."

It was still so early that my voice sounded hoarse when I objected. "You think I'm a traveller?" I asked, then examined my clothes — jeans and a plain white T-shirt.

She smiled and whispered, "Compared to most Turkish people, you are lacking some colour."

I know that she meant sun — my skin was paler than hers — but I felt like she was really talking about my soul. I looked closely at her. She might have been younger than me. Her sandals were broken, nails unclean, dark patches on her skin. Her lips had cracked from dryness. The child looked like he was in much better condition. His clothes were dirty, too, but his skin was smooth and he was otherwise well kept.

His hair was messy and he looked sleepy, but who wouldn't be a little tired at nearly seven in the morning? Clearly, the woman took better care of the boy than herself. She seemed exhausted, as if she had sat on the edge of this sidewalk for many years, always offering nice words to strangers and expecting nothing in return. I must have been examining her for too long because she spoke as if she could read my mind.

"My child is my greatest treasure," she said, kissing his forehead. "We appreciate your generosity. I feel happy as long as he is happy. I am fed if he is fed. We are blessed. Please, continue with your travelling, we will keep you no longer. The ferry awaits."

I felt compelled to hug her, to soothe her, to give her my shoes, so that at least her feet would be comfortable. It is possible that she was genuinely content with her life, having her son by her side, but to me it looked like she had little. Perhaps I am the greedy person here, wanting something more than just a warm house and food on my table.

I bent down and looked directly into her tired eyes. "Please, take care of yourself," I encouraged softly.

She reached out and squeezed my forearm. "Thank you. And good luck."

I fought back the desire to take her with me on a tour of İstanbul, but it felt like something she would refuse. Letting go of my arm, she tilted her head toward the ferry terminal, urging me to go. I waved goodbye to her son. When I got to the end of the street, I turned back to see the boy eating the fig. She wiped the juices from around the edge of his mouth and proceeded to bury his giggles with cheek kisses.

• • •

Crisp, salty air filled my lungs with every breath. The coast was a welcoming sight. The Bosphorus Strait, where two continents meet, had always been one of my favourite places. If only these waters could speak, they would tell a million stories. Tales of battles and bloodshed, comedy and tragedy. History was made on these waters. Its edges glowed with the clearest shade of turquoise. Reflections of small stone houses and green oak trees lined the end of the docks. The deep blue current led the way for a cargo ship passing under the Fatih Sultan Mehmet Bridge. I barely resisted diving in after it. The sky was quickly hinting at pale blue, and not one cloud stained the canvas above.

The skyline was quite unfamiliar. Skyscrapers had been built between mosques and red-tiled houses, while electrical wires towered above the flag poles that adorned the cliffside. When I was a child, buildings were sparse and the trees had room to grow. Now, there was barely any space for a single flower to bloom among the towering structures. I was a little disappointed that the city had developed so much while I was away. Looking to its horizon, only the bridges were unchanged.

In this city, its roads flooded with cars, a suspension bridge stitched Europe and Asia together. The bridge was always overcome with traffic, the sounds of the water below drowned by the cacophony of horns and engines. İstanbul never sleeps.

The large car ferry headed for İstinye was waiting at the port, and some passengers were already boarding. The crowd was made up of mostly young boys in school uniforms but also a few well-dressed professionals. Surprisingly, they were all quite noisy this morning, shouting on their cellphones about scheduling a meeting and ranting about long work hours until finally taking a breath to call the çaycı over from across the boardwalk. The schoolboys were especially rowdy, shoving each other, laughing and yelling insults. A boy with a stockier build pushed one of his friends into an elderly man. Stumbling, the old man dropped a small piece of paper but managed to grab the boat's handrail to keep from falling.

"Çocuklar!" the man shouted angrily. "Dikkat! What are you doing?"

Ignoring the old man's yelling, the boys crammed onto the narrow staircase and raced to the top-floor seating area. The boy who got to the top of the painted stairs first told his friends to keep running to avoid being reprimanded a second time. I went to the old man and helped him pick up the paper off the ground. I noticed it read "Timur Karga," with a Kavacık address on the letterhead. I handed it to him, and he stuffed the paper into his pocket.

"How disruptive they are, and dangerous!" Amca yelled to the air. "These children are really going to hurt someone one of these days. Will they never learn?"

"Unfortunately, they are a little overexcited this morning," I said.

"Terbiyesizler," he mumbled.

I helped him to a nearby seat, leaning his cane on the bench next to him.

"You're one of the good ones." He gestured to the çaycı for two ajda glasses, so I took it as a sign and sat down next to him. "Are you from Beykoz?"

"Y-Yes," I said hesitantly. "I've been away for a long time, but I've returned for my sister's wedding." The old man nodded gently, like he'd heard me tell this story before.

"Most of our youth are leaving these days," he said with some misery in his voice. "May your sister have a blessed life."

"Thank you, Amca."

Hunched over, Timur Amca looked as if he was carrying something heavy. The old man was barely able to lift his arm to place three liras on the tea boy's tray. He seemed tired as he rubbed his reddened eyes with one hand, holding onto the scorching glass with the other. The morning air felt a little chilly on the ferry, but the hot tea was soothing.

"It is quite early, isn't it, Amca?" I said softly. "I needed another hour of sleep, I think."

"Sleep is important. Without rest, you will age quickly." Timur Amca smirked. "It is too late for me, but you have some time still." He quickly scanned my face and added, "Perhaps, you should get some sun, too."

I raised an eyebrow. "Are you also saying that I'm too pale?"

"Also? There have been others who have told you this?" he joked, and we shared a little laugh. We didn't even feel the ferry leave port, only noticed the edge of the pier moving away. "Dressed like that, you are not heading to the wedding now?"

"No," I replied. "It's happening tomorrow. I'm just running some errands today."

"Kolay gelsin," Timur Amca expressed with a nod of his head. "I'm having breakfast with my daughter before she goes to work. We're meeting at the Cınaraltı Café in Emirgan — you know the one?"

An image of my father flashed into my mind. I must have been a toddler, because in my memory he was holding my tiny hand as we crossed the street, heading into the garden of a restaurant that overlooked the water. The patio was overwhelmed by a towering tree with a large pale trunk. He pointed at it and said, "This is one of the oldest trees in the city! Let's sit under it and enjoy some sweets." But before I knew it, the image had once more faded from my mind.

"I think so," I told the old man. "Isn't that a famous café?"

Timur Amca seemed ready to collapse from weariness, but he tried to point in the vague direction of the restaurant.

"When she was a little girl," he began. "I used to take my daughter there sometimes, after classes. The café was close to her school and my work."

"You were a teacher?"

"A doctor," he corrected. "I worked at the hospital nearby, researching. That was over forty years ago."

He reminded me of the beggar woman I'd passed on my way to the port. Timur Amca probably spent his whole life rescuing people and had barely received any thanks in return. Naturally, he was tired. Exhaustion seemed to be the longest-running trend in İstanbul.

"Thank you, Amca. I'm sure Türkiye is grateful for your work."

He looked off toward the bridge, his mouth forced into a straight line.

I continued, "And I'm sure your daughter will be happy to see you."

"I'm afraid not," he said solemnly. "I don't have good news to give her."

He sounded so defeated that I didn't want to press it further, but my curiosity got the better of me.

"What do you mean?" I asked. He didn't meet my eyes, but he spoke clearly.

"My wife passed away three days ago," he admitted. "My daughter hasn't been told yet."

Despite sipping on hot tea, the air that filled my lungs seemed colder than ever. For a moment, I contemplated moving to the covered part of the ferry, where the seats were behind glass. I decided against it. A cool breeze felt appropriate.

"Başınız sağolsun," I said delicately. I had forgotten that I knew those words.

"Thank you." His gaze was downcast. "No matter how many times I hear that phrase, it still comforts me. She was very sick, my wife, for many years."

His voice grew calm and quiet, as if confessing a secret that he had long ago accepted. I had the sudden need to hold his hand.

"Her body eventually gave up," he added. "But to be honest, her mind had been lost to us a long time ago. It doesn't feel like she died recently."

"What was her condition?" I almost whispered.

"The cause of death was attributed to her heart, but she had suffered from panic disorders and dissociation for the last few years, since first starting treatment." He sighed deeply. It seemed to me like he was waging an internal argument about whether or not to elaborate further.

After a moment, he added, "I blame myself. I was trying to save her body, but it was at the cost of her mind. I kept pushing new treatments that I found through research.

I should have just listened to what she wanted. She was constantly afraid."

I placed a hand on his forearm and found the muscle there to be strong. For a man with wrinkled skin, he felt like stone. I stared into my tea as I spoke.

"You were only trying to help. I'm sure you had the best of intentions," I replied. "I really am sorry. It must have been very difficult to watch her endure that pain."

"Loss never gets easier, no matter how practiced we may be," he told me sadly.

Timur Amca patted my hand, which was resting on his forearm. I followed his gaze up, to the cawing of a crow above. The horizon was now a uniform colour.

Swinging his head back down in defeat, he spoke more to himself than to me. "Why is the sky turning blue?" he grumbled. "Didn't it get the message? We have to mourn today."

We stayed sitting quietly for a couple of minutes more as we finished our tea. I thought about this man's wife. To be trapped inside your own mind is terrifying. It is a prison of your own making, one that is both consuming and self-harming. Pain is especially hurtful when it is intangible, because people do not usually recognize pain that doesn't leave scars and bruises. How can we receive care and begin the process of healing when we cannot understand the scope and impact of our pain? Pain can be hidden among someone's awards and in the pride they feel for their accomplishments.

Pain might sting our eyes as we stare at the egg we dropped on the floor. How do we know that it's pain if we can still laugh on cue? For me, pain fuelled itself in the shadows of my bedroom late at night, then quietly raged through my mind during the day as I carried on with life. The way that pain decides to show up is not a choice that we can make. Most people can't understand the legitimacy of pain when they can't see it themselves — it's not always something you can X-ray.

About five years ago, I was in a bad state, too. I was irritable and angry all the time. I pushed people away. I had meltdowns. My own mind was my enemy, to the point where I had become a major threat to my own health. There was so much that I was worried about, and no one seemed to care as much as I did. They didn't understand, and I didn't have it in me to begin explaining it to them. After some concerned remarks from my sister about my behaviour, I realized these feelings were not random. I didn't know how to stop them on my own, but I knew who to ask.

I went to a therapist to try and understand what I was feeling. For the first few sessions, I was afraid to talk, because whenever I tried to explain myself, I would start to cry. I didn't get why, and that only made me more embarrassed. It seems a little ridiculous now, because obviously therapists are meant to assist you, but I just didn't know how she could possibly help. It took a couple of weeks, but she managed to convince me to talk. She said that my body naturally sweats when I work my muscles, so crying was like working the muscles of my soul. Apparently, my soul needed more exercise. I started to tell her little stories about myself. I would still cry when I did, but at least I was able to complete a few sentences before reaching for the tissues. Soon, I was talking more about myself than I ever had. She not only heard me, but she listened. I was truly thankful, as she gave me what I really needed: to have someone acknowledge that I was feeling pain. This acknowledgement went a long way, but it was hard to put all of that overwhelm into individual words. The phrase "I understand you" became the greatest sound to me. She gave me a couple of techniques to use whenever I felt the negative thoughts threatening to resurface. They still help, but my anxiety isn't the issue anymore. Now, I need to address the void that has been slowly eating me up inside, making my life bland.

My thoughts returned to the ferry as the tea boy came back around to gather our glasses. Before I could help him, the older man grabbed his cane and was getting up to leave. The ferry had docked at the opposite port, and people were already disembarking. I helped the man down the steel stairs, watching the loud schoolboys race past the other passengers and toward the bus stop outside the İstinye Ferry Terminal.

"Çocuğum," Timur Amca began. "You are kind to listen to an old man. I thank you for your company and your comforting words." He gave me two pats on the upper arm.

"Rica ederim, Amca," I said and returned the pats. "I wish you and your daughter well."

He turned away with a gentle smile and started limping toward the awaiting taxis.

Retracing the path of the young boys, I found myself waiting at the Tersane bus stop. A string of colourful buses arrived. I boarded a shiny new one with "40T" running along its digital banner. The bus was hot and full, most of its passengers dressed for work. Earphones on blast and eyes glued to their phones, people would hop on and off the bus after just a couple of stops. Standing at the very back, I gripped the handrail as the bus swung around corners, following the curvature of the coastline. Among the packed crowd, my cheeks were flushed red as we travelled to the first stop of my day trip. Excitement bubbled in my chest again as I watched the Bosphorus, a blur outside my window.

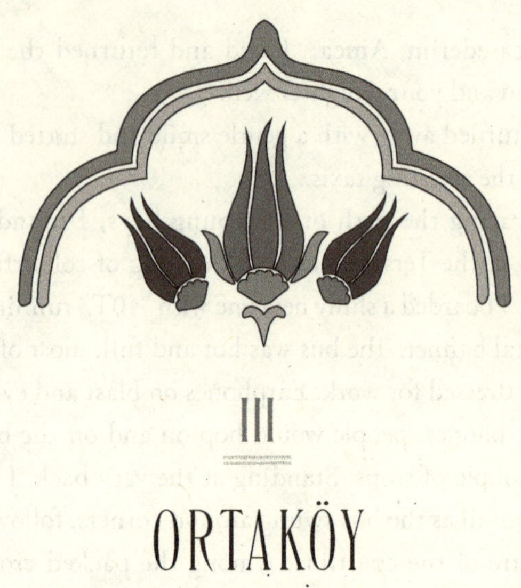

III

ORTAKÖY

It wasn't long before the bus arrived in Ortaköy. The little district was full of winding, narrow alleyways lined with bazaars and coffee shops. It was always busy there, even if it was raining — much of the alleys were covered with hanging sheets that acted as tents. The Bosphorus waves dulled the chatter the closer one got to the ferry port. Growing up, my family and I would come to Ortaköy often, mostly because it was such an easy trip from our house. Nergiz and I would stop at every vendor's stall, practising our haggling and still overspending despite our efforts. Among the merchandise, we thought we might find rare antiques worth millions, so we searched for candidates and excitedly compared notes. As we grew older, our attention turned to stylish workbags and books — that is, if we didn't get sidetracked by all the stalls selling fried foods. My parents were entertained, too, and would usually look for gifts to buy their friends and colleagues in Canada. There were rows upon rows of shiny handcrafted goods, and sitting on each table's edge was a cat acting like a bodyguard for the merchandise. Whether I was sampling freshly squeezed orange juice, taking a picture by the shoreline, or bartering over a hookah bottle of a colour that I didn't yet own, I never missed a single corner of the marketplace.

Once you made it out of the maze of pathways, you came upon a tremendous view of the water and one of the oldest mosques in the city. Modest in size, the white building was adorned with elaborate baroque and neoclassical detailing, making it one of the prettiest in İstanbul. I loved that the mosque would catch and reflect whatever colours filled the sky, turning it purple, orange, or stormy blue, depending on the day. The mosque and surrounding pier could be found on most souvenirs — coasters, posters, bags; whatever you were looking for, there would always be a design available with Ortaköy printed on it. The signature scene of a towering white dome and elaborate matching fence with a view of the bridge behind it. The view was stunning in all kinds of weather and at any time of day. Countless tourists and locals flocked there no matter the season, taking pictures, positioning themselves in the same orientation as on the merchandise. Our photo albums back home contained so many pictures of my sister and me posing in these very spots. If you compiled all our photos, you could probably make one of those flip books where you see us gradually growing up as you move through the pictures. Whenever we came here, we always left with a full stomach and a couple of nice presents. I remember how thrilled I was one time to take home some embroidered cushion covers for my living room. I was so thrilled, in fact, that I went looking for them again the following year to get other designs. I recalled how my mother would walk around the marketplace until her legs were swollen, but the entire way home, she would have the brightest smile on her face. For days after, she would show off her latest jewellery to her friends and sisters, asking them to guess how much of a discount she managed to get for each piece. In my memories, Ortaköy was always a good time.

Roaming the marketplace now, I came across tables and tables of goods to choose from. I had a hard time resisting buying every single item as I perused wallets, mosaic lamps, and even a rug hanging from the ceiling inside one of the narrow stores. Almost shoulder to shoulder with locals and tourists alike, every person's eyes were darting from one table to the next. The mood was energetic and had an urgency to it, as if the merchandise could sell out at any time. Merchants called out their prices, asked me to buy from them, tried to convince me that their merchandise was better than their neighbour's. It was loud and chaotic, but I enjoyed it. It was as if, through this sea of people and voices, I was not anything special, and that was somewhat comforting. I have never been happy when there are too many eyes on me.

"Arkadaş! Gel gel gelllllll. The best stuff is right in front of you!" shouted a middle-aged man who was gesturing at me, trying to get me to approach his table of belts and other leather goods.

"Yok yok, look here! I have the most satisfied customers. People always complain about Ateş," yelled a blonde woman two tables over. Seated on a plastic stool, she was surrounded by similar merchandise. She didn't even look up at me but instead grinned down at the strap of a leather bag that she was hand-sewing.

"What are you talking about, Yağmur?" shouted Ateş, his face all red and sweaty. "You've gotten delusional in your old age! No one says bad things about me!"

"Yeah, yeah," Yağmur teased. "Then why does your wife always complain to me about you when we get together for tea?"

"Allahallah, you're just making things up." Ateş's mouth twitched with the slightest of smiles. I began to think that these two must bicker with each other to keep their day-to-day entertaining but also to draw attention to their stalls. I learned a long time ago to stay clear of salespeople that were too smart.

Turning down the next street, I stumbled upon the characteristic artist walkway. The alley was lined with reproduction paintings of old İstanbul in hand-carved wooden frames, railway posters of the Orient Express printed on enlarged foam boards, famous actors illustrated on refrigerator magnets, boxes and boxes of records with a mix of Western singers and an eski türkü selection, and even a table advertising multilingual novels for sale. Thinking back, this street was likely the reason I spent so much time in Ortaköy growing up.

Chatter surrounded me as people of all types browsed the various stalls, excited about art and literature that was both old and new. To my right, I overheard two elementary school students asking around for charcoal and drawing paper. To my left, an elderly man was sitting on the curb, carefully examining the index at the back of a biology textbook. There were even two young men playing on their guitar and darbuka under the canopy of a corn seller. Across from them, a little girl was getting a caricature drawn of her. It was nice to see so many people gathered in a single space, bonding over similar interests. I felt a part of this makeshift community of art lovers. We were all happily coexisting in an alley in the middle of İstanbul. I have often thought that art is the dinner table that brings the whole world to sit together.

Before I could stop it, my body started drifting slowly toward a stall set up with black-and-white postcards. On the table was a mahogany box full of old Ottoman Empire stamps and coins. My fingertips grazed over the silver. Picking up one of the coins, I investigated the engravings on it. The seller must have seen me through the window, because he popped his head out through the shop's doorframe suddenly. He was a very thin man with a scruffy beard and bald spots here and there. He stared at my hand, almost lighting it on fire with his gaze.

"Are you going to buy it or just keep making it dirty?" he asked casually.

"I'm sorry!" I quickly retracted my hand. "I was just admiring it."

"Your hands have oils on them," he said bluntly. "You will tarnish the silver."

"I'm sorry," I said again, embarrassed.

The man stepped down from the doorframe and joined me at the table. He picked up the coin that I was holding and removed a red cloth from his pocket. He expertly polished the coin before putting it back in the box with the others. My eyes slid to the postcards again. I was determined to buy one but was feeling too ashamed to ask the price.

After polishing a second coin, the seller followed me to the end of the table and held up a black-and-white postcard of the Galata Bridge.

"You can't find this one anywhere else," he said confidently. "Only ten of them were sold, and I'm quite sure the museums have the rest boxed up in their basements."

I hadn't seen the postcard before, but I wasn't sure if he was telling the truth. I wondered how he could have acquired the postcard if it was so rare. I looked to another one, a photo of an Üsküdar ferry boat with handrails on the upper deck and a large back propeller at its rear. All the old ferry boats from when I was a child had been replaced with a sleeker, more modern design. I missed the old ones; they used to look like actual boats, complete with gusts of wind that tunnelled through the lookout railings, cooling down passengers on a hot summer day. Now the ferries looked like some kind of spaceship, the İstanbul cityscape muted by the dark tinted window glass.

The seller picked up the postcard that I pointed to and handed it to me to examine. "This one is a modern reproduction," he said. "Only ten liras. It's in the best condition."

Holding the postcard, I remembered what it was like being a child at the Üsküdar Ferry Terminal, seeing the ferries towering above me and smelling the diesel. My father told me about how they used to pump steam and how when he was my age, he would watch the workers shovel coal into the ferry engines. Apparently, the old ferries would blow their horn before leaving port, a booming but not alarming sound. He also told me that the captains would use the horn to make a quick *whoop-whoop* sound whenever they passed a friend's house on the Bosphorus, cuing the homeowner to step outside for a quick wave. Scanning the passenger carriers all lined up along the harbour, I could see how each of them were going to a different destination, their banners outlining their travel route. There were huge crowds, all bunched together and leaning on the closed gate. As soon as the ferry docked and released its passengers, the attendant opened the inner gate and the crowds rushed forward. Amid the pushing and shoving, I recalled my sister holding my hand, pulling me along with her. My father was ahead of us, clearing a path with his wide shoulders, and my mother was guiding me from behind. We boarded the boat, and my father led us to the second floor and claimed a spot on the outer bench that would fit us all. Without any discussion, we all turned our attention to the sea. We watched as some passengers threw bread pieces to the seagulls flying close to the ferry. During these short trips, my father would always point out all the major parts of the city as we passed them. Every now and then, he would take a photo of us with a different landmark in the background. I remember how my sister would always pout, annoyed by how many times she would have to pose for the camera. Reflecting, I had a good guess as to how she would treat her wedding photographer.

I took out two bills from my pocket and handed them to the seller. He put the postcard in a little white paper bag, which I slid into my back pocket. We wished each other good day, and I headed back toward the labyrinth of alleyways. After just a couple of minutes, the sun started to feel too hot, my stomach too empty. I hadn't eaten a proper breakfast, and it was well into the morning at this point — I needed a decent meal. Knowing that most of the restaurants were by the water, I used the minarets of Ortaköy's mosque as my guide and returned to the port.

There were long lineups outside the restaurants at the port, but I spotted a popular kumpir stall that was serving customers rather quickly. Lining up behind a mother and her child, I watched as the woman struggled to keep hold of her son's hand. Twisting and tugging, the little boy ripped his hand free from her grasp and went running after some pigeons that were busy eating pieces of corn off the ground. Whenever the pigeons landed, the boy would chase them off. His mother sighed deeply and just stared at him as he ran back and forth. After his fifth time doing this, the pigeons scattered toward the food stall, and one of the birds flew too closely to the customer at the front of the line. The man whipped his head around to the rest of the line, seeking out the parent of the child. Humiliated, the mother of the boy called out to her son.

"Osman!" she shouted. "Come here, now!"

"No!" the boy called from across the courtyard.

"You're being a bother to everyone. Leave the birds alone." The mother was annoyed. The food stall line moved ahead a couple steps.

"No!" Osman yelled again, his plump cheeks growing increasingly pink.

"Don't make me repeat myself." There was an edge to her voice now.

Short of breath, he replied, "But I want to … know how … they fly!"

"Ne?" she said angrily.

Osman didn't take the hint but instead spoke more loudly, as if his mother simply didn't hear him the first time. "I want to know how they fly!" he yelled. "Why can't I have wings? I want wings!"

"You can't have wings, you're not a bird. Now get over here." She pointed to her own two feet. The line ahead of her began moving again.

"Why can't I be a bird?" Osman said to himself. "Can I *get* a bird at least?" He wandered back to his mother's side, frustrated.

"Do you want a beating instead? I said, come here!" She grabbed his elbow as soon as the boy was within reach. He cried out at the sudden yank of his arm and proceeded to avoid his mother's gaze. She spoke to him in a low, threatening voice.

"Do not disrespect me, Osman," she seethed. "Do you hear me? You have to do what I say." She spoke forcefully and didn't let go of his arm.

"Annecim, acıtıyorsun," he protested.

"You should have come when I called you. I will not repeat myself."

Osman remained silent and stood obediently at his mother's side, sweat dripping from the tips of his short hair. It occurred to me how a child has the ability to see a complicated world in such an uncomplicated way. As I grow older, I have frequently found myself reflecting on how a child's way of thinking is a blessing. Children are knowledgeable enough to ask questions in order to get to know the world around them. They are ripe for learning. As an adult, I feel like I might have lost some of that freedom to wonder. I think too rationally, and it takes away from the excitement of not knowing. Quite simply, Osman liked birds because they could fly. Osman also wanted to fly and to learn how it was done. He might also have been confused as to why his mother was so angry with him and the birds. That was it. There was nothing more for him to think about.

Osman didn't think about how the birds were scattering because they were scared of him. He wasn't aware of his mother's embarrassment when he sent the pigeons flying toward a customer who then turned around in anger. He didn't notice everyone in line criticizing his mother's parenting methods. He hadn't realized that he would now have to wander around İstanbul in sweaty clothes until he returned home. These were the thoughts of an adult, not a little boy. Osman was still new and transparent to the world. He was a clear thinker, led only by his curiosity. He was free to explore his own mind and all that was around him, untouched from experiences that hadn't scarred him yet. My own mind was quite far from Osman's. Mine had become cloudy and thundering.

If only everyone could maintain a child's level of rawness and simplicity as they grow older, we might be able to see life more freely for what it is.

I was a fairly obedient child. I might have had some hiccups during my preteen years, when I pushed back against my parents and sister — as you do when hormones are coursing through your body. As a teen, it was harder to peer pressure me into breaking rules because I often felt scared and burdened, like I would be letting down my whole family if I got caught. I knew my reputation was at stake. Allah forbid, my grandfather found out about my wrongdoings, or my grandmother, or any family member for that matter. Their opinion was too important to me; I loved them deeply and would probably trade all of my surface-level relationships to spend more time with just one of my elders. So, to show my affection, I was rather well behaved. I was practised. I didn't seek mischief; troublemakers actually made me uncomfortable. Reflecting on it now, this personality trait might have been why I have had a harder time keeping friends.

We build friendships by trusting each other, and whenever I have made a new friend, they have naturally tested my trust. Rarely were my childhood friendships built on an understanding that was gentle and truthful and accepting.

Usually, it depended on if I allowed myself to be treated as less than I deserved, or how malleable I could be, to fit in with the rest of them. Sometimes, those friends distanced themselves from me because I wouldn't play along, or they would get me in trouble if I did. There were exceptions, of course, and I've got some great friends now, but back then is when I stopped trusting most people. I still consider a breach of trust to be one of the harshest acts a person could commit. I'm not sure if it's an attribute of being a child of immigrants, but I have considered it my responsibility, to myself and my family, to keep up my good behaviour despite the challenges that I've faced.

I wonder sometimes if my family ever appreciated my efforts.

Once it was my turn at the food stall, I topped the baked potato with some feta and dill yogurt, chopped black olives, and sliced cucumbers. Noticing the redness of the merchant's face, I tipped him a little extra, pitying him for having to work under the sun for hours at a time. I took large strides toward the comfort of the shade, leaning on the edge of a nearby stone wall to eat my snack. Across the courtyard, I saw Osman's mother leading her son away to eat his food from a bench where he would not bother the pigeons.

My stomach settled a little now that I had eaten, but I had a craving for caffeine. It was mid-morning, the typical time for Turkish coffee. I remembered liking a coffee shop that was right on the water, and so I went in pursuit of a relaxing drink.

After turning a couple of corners, I found that my favourite café had built a new extension. They'd renovated part of the old building, adding a large awning to one side and doubling the seating space underneath. Climbing hanımeli vines perfumed the far corners of the patio. The inside was full of scrap wood, scaffolding, and the sound of hammering. The outside seating was pretty busy, but I spotted one available table. As I approached the podium by the entrance, a waiter in a white ironed shirt and black apron greeted me with a nod.

"Bir kişilik, lütfen," I said timidly.

"Oh! You're Turkish," he replied with wide eyes. He grabbed a menu from under the podium and gestured to the patio. "This way." He started toward the free table.

For a brief moment, I contemplated getting my coffee to go. That way I could drink it in the sun and tan my pale skin in a desperate effort to look more like a local. Thinking again about the sweat dripping down my spine and my belly full of potato, I decided against it and followed the waiter to a shady spot on the patio. Sitting right next to a potted baby lemon tree, I rubbed its leaves in my hand and inhaled its fresh citrus scent. Time for my first little break.

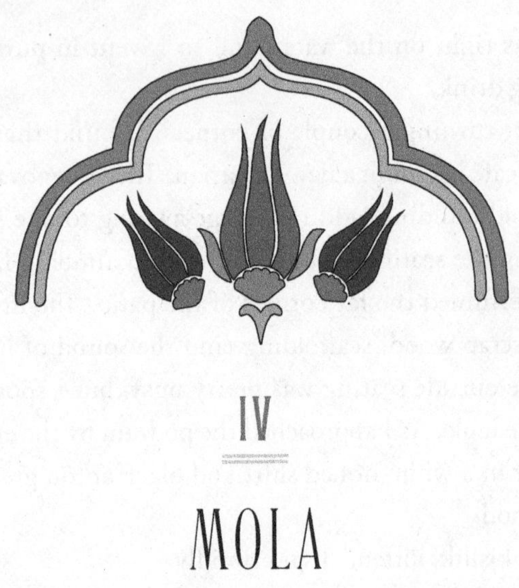

IV

MOLA

I didn't need to see the menu but still pretended I was considering other options. I knew what I was going to order. Glancing at the empty chair across from me, I played with some lemon leaves that had fallen onto the table. Looking around, there were mostly tables of two people and just one family, all of us seated out on the patio. At a quick glance, there were two young men at one table, not speaking to each other as they looked out onto the water, lost in their own thoughts. They had finished drinking their tea. Dressed quite stylishly, each wore a pair of expensive sunglasses perched atop their heads. Their phones were on the table, facing down. Sitting in a safe silence, without any pressure to hold conversation or entertain the other, I wondered if this comfort was a testament to a long relationship or a strong one.

Behind one of them sat a woman and another man who occasionally burst into laughter. The woman had very curly hair that was turning frizzy in the heat, and her iced lemonade was still full to the brim. She was telling what seemed to be a vivid story, waving her arms with theatrical gestures, while the man seated across from her looked on, completely enthralled by his companion, his iced Americano untouched. I love storytellers and felt a pull to be a part of their conversation, but I think a third person would have disrupted their balance. So I stayed in my chair, sitting in my curiosity, wanting to know if the tale was genuinely an exciting one or if the woman was just making it worth listening to.

Next to them, a woman in a navy-blue hijab with delicate lavender embroidery sat quietly and nodded to the man sharing her table. He spoke tenderly, as if discussing serious matters. She didn't look at him, instead using her fork to play with the decadent piece of carrot cake on the table between them. She kept her eyebrows slightly furrowed and never once ate from her fork. Whatever he was saying, I think she had lost her appetite in hearing it. I would hope that someone wouldn't let me order any food if they knew they had to tell me uncomfortable news — a full stomach would make me feel sick. I certainly did not long to join their table.

The family seated together at one table was composed of several generations. A little girl with fine chestnut hair sat on a heavier woman's lap. Bouncing up and down on the woman's knee, the girl giggled repeatedly. A very thin teenage boy, seemingly unaware of his surroundings, sat between the bouncing girl and his mother, playing a racing game on his phone. He swayed to the sides as he turned a virtual wheel, sometimes bumping in to his mother's arm while she carried on, quietly sipping her latte. At the same table, a man with greying hair was having a mild argument with another man in his later years. The older gentleman twirled his black cane as he listened, expertly making calm counterarguments throughout the discussion. With so many personalities seated together, they made up a complete household. I wondered how many troubles they've overcome together over the years and if those obstacles ended up making it any easier to maintain healthy and lasting bonds between them.

A waitress wearing fitted black dress pants and a clean white collared shirt approached me, eying the other tables as she passed through the patio space. She had light brown hair pulled into a tight bun and looked to be in her mid-twenties.

"Hello, welcome. Have you decided on what to order?" she asked pleasantly. I noticed her nametag — Ece. "Perhaps just a drink order, if you're still deciding on food?"

"No, I'm ready," I answered. "I'll take one Turkish coffee, please. Orta."

"Is that all?" she asked automatically.

I paused, surprised. I expected her to ask a different question. When I make Turkish coffee for my friends, I always have to explain to them the different levels of sweetness on offer. There are special terms to use when ordering Turkish coffee — plain, medium, a little sweet, very sweet. Not to mention that making that particular type of coffee is an art and takes some practice. Among Turks, people are often judged by the quality of their coffee-making skills. We get especially excited to tell fortunes with the coffee grounds, but there is more to it — it's all in the process. When I have made it for my friends in Toronto, they don't stop to appreciate the amount of foam at the top of every cup. They don't comment on how well I've served their coffee, never spilling a single drop. They don't know what it all means, and they don't think to ask. Really, I don't blame them. Why would they pay attention to such small details in a single cup of coffee? Still, I have always loved and savoured Turkish coffee for that very reason — not because of its bitter taste, but because of all its unsaid meanings. It had been a long time since someone had understood those hidden messages without me having to explain them. When the waitress didn't hesitate at my order, I felt like she knew what I meant by it, like we had shared a secret language. I was overthinking things again, I realized.

I handed the menu back and thanked her.

"I'll get it right away," Ece said, smiling. She turned on her heel and headed back inside the restaurant. I noticed that the mother sitting at the family table glanced at the waitress as she left but didn't call after her.

Sitting in the shade and under a fan, the breeze started to cool me down right away. I was grateful for the mola, knowing that I had a long day ahead of me. I continued playing with the leaves that had fallen on the table, thinking about my post-coffee destination. I decided almost immediately that I would head to the busier side of İstanbul next. In this heat, I'd have to take another bus. The metro would have been faster, but I wanted to see the Galata Bridge, and maybe even enjoy the view from Galata Tower.

The waitress returned with my coffee and placed it on the table. Expertly brewed, thick foam on top, prettily presented in a traditional İznik cup. Red tulips with turquoise and gold motifs decorated the porcelain. A single piece of a greenish lokum sat on the plate. It was a double-churned pistachio flavour, which was my absolute favourite kind. I decided to save it for last, to end my coffee on a happy note instead of eating it right away. I took one sip, pooling the coffee on my tongue for a bit before swallowing. There was a hint of sweetness, but the coffee was still strong and very warm. It tasted like home. Ece left again for the kitchen without stopping at any of the other tables.

One of the two men sitting at the far table took his eyes off the sea and turned his attention to the ferry approaching the Ortaköy dock. He asked the other young man a question I couldn't hear, which resulted in a one-word reply. They looked relaxed, watching as passengers disembarked. I sipped more of my coffee and wondered to myself if they had any plans today.

After a few minutes, the woman at the family table stood. Her son didn't look up from his game as his mother left, heading in the direction of the kitchen. A few minutes passed, and she returned with a handful of napkins, which she proceeded to use to wipe the sweat from her son's neck. Her face revealed a look of displeasure. The heavier woman took the child off her lap and placed her on a nearby chair.

"Did something happen?" the heavier woman asked casually, readjusting her dress. I sipped my coffee, expectantly.

The mother reluctantly answered, "They were arguing."

"Who?"

The mother watched as her son ignored the little girl's request to play the racing game. "Our waitress and another guy — the manager, I think."

"About what?"

"I don't know, but she looked exhausted."

The other woman *tsked* in response as she removed a tube of lipstick from her purse. Another minute passed before shouting could be heard inside the restaurant. The words weren't clear, but it was obvious that someone had reached their breaking point. There was gasping between the shouts, as if Ece couldn't decide if she needed to yell or cry. The patio went silent, everyone there listening intently. Even the curly-haired girl stopped telling her story, her arms frozen in the air. The renovating team had stopped hammering. Everyone turned their attention to the voices now booming from inside the restaurant and the two figures who could be seen in the shadow of the entryway. I sipped the last of my coffee.

"Just because I'm struggling doesn't mean that I'm failing!" Ece yelled.

"It looks a lot like failure to me," said the restaurant manager, his voice stern.

"I don't care what you think! I'm working hard! Not for you, or for anyone else, but for me." She dug a finger into her own chest. "How could you treat me so poorly and for so long? I can't take it anymore. I can't believe I managed to stay for so long. You are so selfish!" She wasn't going to back down.

"Who are *you* to criticize *me*?" the manager retaliated. "I gave you a job, but for what? You haven't improved at all. This is the third time you've asked for a pay increase. What exactly are these *goals* of yours that require me to keep being so generous, despite your lack of skill?" His thick voice was sounding venomous.

"I don't have to explain myself to you." Ece's words caught in her throat. The manager huffed in response. "It's none of your business. I have a plan that's going to take me to better places. I don't need you. I will surpass my own expectations and do it all by myself. I will even surpass the ridiculous bar that other people set for me. I refuse to believe that *this* is as good as it gets!" She said that last part while gesturing to the construction zone around her.

"You expect to travel the world on a waitress's salary?" The manager's sarcasm was biting. "You will get nowhere. How useless you are."

"What I do with my life and my money are not your concern!" she shouted. "All I ask is that you pay me properly! I work harder than anyone."

"I will not pay you a penny more. You're just a waitress. You will get a waitress's salary, and at the time that you deserve it. You think too highly of yourself."

People approached the restaurant's entrance, curious, trying to look inside to locate the source of the yelling, but they were turned away by the host. There weren't any available seats on the patio, anyway.

Ece's voice rang clear. "I've been here for three years," she shouted. "If you can't appreciate what I've sacrificed for this place, then I'm leaving!" Her voice was starting to give out.

The manager switched to a more controlled tone, as if Ece wasn't the first waitress to publicly argue with him. "Good luck with that," he countered. "There are many people who would give everything to have your job. You should be grateful to me."

"I can't believe what I'm hearing!" she yelled. He smirked in return. Ece untied her apron and threw it onto a sawdust-covered table. "I bet you don't even understand how much I do for this place. You won't make it without me. And if I can put up with your bullshit for this long, I'll survive anywhere." She stared at him, enunciating her last words. "I'm done!"

The manager stared back, arms crossed. "You have to give me two weeks' notice if you want to quit." He sounded tired. "Take your break now, instead of later. I'll have some forms for you to sign at the end of the day."

The manager marched back into his small office, mumbling to himself. He slammed the door. The staff exchanged glances, concerned by the public argument. One of the other waitresses approached Ece and placed a gentle hand on her shoulder.

"Have a seat on the patio," the waitress told Ece. "Get some fresh air. I'll bring you something to drink."

Ece watched the ground, tears refusing to stream. She turned toward the patio and looked up to find that every person at every table was watching her, whispering among themselves as they stared. I didn't envy Ece. A room full of people with me at the centre of attention always made me so uncomfortable. Nergiz was the same, I knew, because we had commiserated about this topic before. In Canada, we grew up trying to blend in so that we could make friends with the born-and-raised Canadian kids. But anytime we stood out as different from them in any way was a point against us. Any behaviours that suggested we were still Turkish would earn us an unwanted platform for scrutiny. Too many eyes, too many opinions. I'm sure Ece felt embarrassed for having argued so loudly and so personally in front of the customers. I felt like she needed someone to take care of her, to maybe offer up a hug or some encouraging words.

I waved at Ece and caught her attention. I gestured to the empty seat in front of me. "Please," I said. She hesitated but made her way to my table, probably eager to not be the centre of attention any longer. She brushed the leaves from the seat and then sat down on the delicate chair. Her cheeks and forehead appeared flushed.

"You don't have to talk to me," I said quietly. "But I'll listen, if you want me to."

She looked at me a little wide-eyed, seemingly taken by surprise. When she finally blinked, I saw tears escaping her eyes, gliding down her cheek.

"My break is only fifteen minutes," she said. Her chin started to quiver. She wiped her face. "I just need to rest near a fan, and they're still renovating inside. I'll leave you alone when another table opens up."

"That's your choice," I replied. "But I really don't mind your company."

She nodded, smoothing out the tablecloth with her hands. She took a deep breath and rested her elbows on the table. I watched as she hugged herself loosely. The other customers had stopped staring at her but continued to speak among themselves in hushed tones.

"I am sorry to bother you," she said softly.

"Not at all," I assured her. "Please rest. You worked hard today."

"I work hard every day," she replied bitterly.

She was quiet for a moment. No doubt she was processing the fact that she had just quit her job. She was probably recalculating those big plans of hers. Soon, the wrinkles on her forehead started to relax, and she looked lost in thought.

"What are you thinking about?" I asked.

She offered me a sad smile and waved dismissively. "I was just remembering when the days were long and my time was never wasted," she said solemnly.

"Do you think that waitressing here was a waste of your time?"

"A little bit," she admitted.

The other waitress stepped out onto the patio and quickly located Ece, sitting at my table. She smiled at me before placing down another İznik cup identical to mine.

"Sade," she said. Ece nodded and took a greedy sip of her coffee.

There it was again — the secret language. My mother told me that when I was a toddler, I once dipped my pacifier into her plain Turkish coffee. Apparently, I loved the bitter taste, which was unusual for a small child. I later learned that plain Turkish coffee was not for the faint-hearted but for the warriors among us. It was meant for the people who were ready to take on the world. It was a coffee order that symbolized that you didn't have the time to sit around; you just needed to refuel. As if you were in the middle of a war, determined to survive, and you needed a boost. Plain coffee suited Ece.

The waitress asked about my own cup, but I held it and declined to order another. I waited until we were alone again before speaking.

"I don't think this job was a waste of your time," I said to Ece. "Waitressing is not about memorizing orders or perfecting your customer service. It's challenging in a different kind of way. I think you learned more about yourself than you realize. Challenges are good for that."

"You sound like you know this feeling." She raised one eyebrow.

"Possibly," I admitted.

"Actually, I don't feel like I've learned much since I was eighteen. If anything, I feel more beaten, more bruised. As if life has kept me in the corner and was able to take a couple of good swings at me." She pulled out her bun and ran her fingers through her hair. "Or maybe it feels more like I'm drowning … Sorry, I'm going on and on."

Ece didn't look at me when she spoke, but I wanted her to keep going. I needed her to feel heard. Perhaps my eagerness to help was a testament to all the times that I wished people had actually listened to me when I was struggling. Often, when feeling low, I've felt a need for sympathy, for unconditional kindness. I don't usually receive it — it's rare in this world — but I have learned to pay attention to those who also long for it. If Ece wanted to tell me the details, she could. I also knew that not everyone could so easily confide in a stranger at a café. But I think that I was starting to understand her. Drowning didn't sound too different from how I was feeling these days.

"But today, you kept your chin up," I replied, trying to sound optimistic.

She finished her coffee with a second sip. "It's hard to keep your chin up when everyone's hand is pushing your head underwater."

"I'm sorry it's so tough for you right now," I replied. "I promise, it won't always be like this. There will be happy moments, good things to look forward to."

"Yeah, yeah, I know. I'm just so done with this."

It seemed in that moment like she wasn't speaking about herself but saying it on my behalf — like those words had been tattooed on my forehead and she was just reading them aloud. Like me, like the retired doctor on the ferry — Ece suffered the same as we did. She was surviving life, rather than living it.

Her voice was more passionate now. "I face challenges all the time," she started. "I fight hard. I give and I give and I give, and then I look at myself, only to find that there's no more blood in my veins, no breath left in my lungs. I've sacrificed it all." She looked around, watching for listening customers. She continued, quieter now. Angry. "It takes everything from me. Every time. Always fighting back — it's starting to wear me down. If I have to keep going like this …"

I couldn't help myself from scrunching my eyebrows — I was starting to feel concerned for her.

She gripped herself tighter. "I just want to know when the struggles will end," she said. "I'm so tired. I'm really just so tired."

That sounded right. When it comes to living life, we often lose our motivation if we get beaten down too often. Just when things are looking better, an obstacle gets in the way. Sometimes the hurdles are welcomed, like a distraction or an exciting plot twist. Sometimes we trip over them, scraping ourselves, coming out of the experience more damaged than expected. To top it off, everyone expects us to keep moving forward, despite those deep cuts and bruises. It's hard.

I kept my voice low. "I don't think those struggles will ever end," I told her. "Honestly, I think that might be the whole point. The definition of life."

She nodded and then shrugged, defeated. There were no more comments to make on the topic. We are all born into a life, whether we want it or not — into a contract that we are never even asked to sign. If only we had a movie trailer for life, a way for us to see exactly what the whole show is all about before we decide to play a part. To perform. A strong supporting cast helps and moves the plot along, but it still comes down to the leading role to make it a worthwhile story. Like walking through molasses, my day-to-day life was consistently slow, and my soul felt that resistance. There was no excitement, no sparkling goal to achieve, and I was too tired to push through just for the sake of the show. Considering how worn down and uninterested I'd been feeling for the past few years, my life was seeming more like the tedious second season of a TV show that had started with an intensity it failed to maintain. My only hope was that the episodes would eventually improve. That's where İstanbul came in. This place was my final hope. My last good idea. I was eager to find a fresh outlook, renewed motivation to continue this show on a better note.

Ece then tossed the Turkish delight into her mouth, concluding our conversation. I ate mine, too. The chewy candy stuck to my teeth, slowly dissolving and leaving the softened pistachios behind. The two well-dressed men at the far table stood up, putting some money under an empty tea glass. They thanked the host at the entrance and made their way toward the docks. The curly-haired storyteller at the table next to them was busy looking through her wallet as the man drank his iced Americano in a single go. She placed fifty liras under the half-finished lemonade. When they got up from the table, they were both smiling to themselves. Meanwhile, the family seated together at the table was politely arguing over who would pay. In the end, the older man left some money under the cigarette tray. The little girl ran ahead of everyone, hurrying toward a balloon seller. The young boy's eyes were still glued to his phone — his mother pulled him by the arm, manoeuvring him around chairs and following the girl into the crowd.

Another leaf fell onto the table. Ece got up and pushed her chair in. She leaned on the iron seatback and offered me a small smile.

"Thank you for letting me sit with you," she said. "Your coffee is on me."

"No, my friend," I replied quickly. "This one is on me."

"You really don't have to do that. I feel bad enough for making a scene and then talking to you about my problems —"

"I insist," I told her and took twenty liras out of my wallet, which I placed on the table. "You should always talk when you have problems. I'm glad I was around to listen."

She nodded, "Kesenize bereket."

She walked back into the restaurant and started speaking with the other waitress, the one who'd brought her the coffee. I stole a fallen yellowish flower from under the table and pressed it into my wallet before leaving the restaurant. For today, Ortaköy was finished with me, so I went looking for the bus stop again.

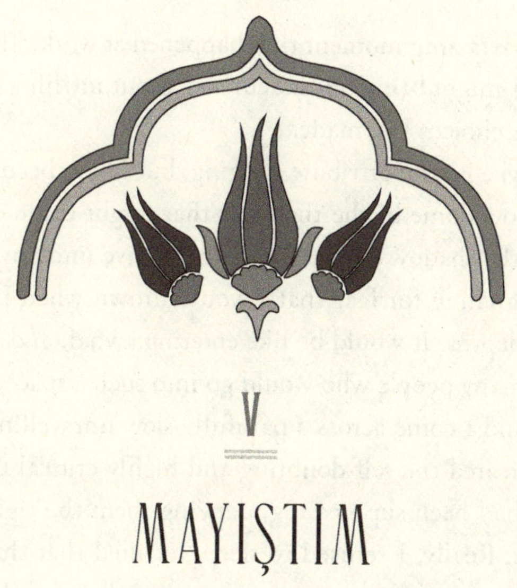

V

MAYIŞTIM

I boarded the 30D bus to Kemeraltı. Despite having drunk strong coffee, the warmth and rocking of the bus as it followed the twists and turns of the road made me drowsy in my seat. I hadn't been sleeping well for a few years — only when I was truly exhausted. I must confess, I've actually been afraid to fall asleep because of what I might see in my nightmares. There is no control in the dreamworld, so my subconscious goes exploring. I might discover corners of my mind that are better left in the dark. I might relive the anxiety I've felt over keeping in touch with friends or replay an embarrassing moment that happened at work. The recollections might bring up insecurities about my life's purpose and the choices I've made.

Maybe it is an attribute of aging, but I have become worried about some of the thoughts that might come creeping out of the shadows. I was reluctant to dive into any further soul-searching for fear that I would drown when I learned of my depths. It would be like entering a void, and I do not know many people who would go into such a space willingly. Would I come across a painfully slow unravelling of the self? I feared the self-doubting and highly critical thoughts that I had been suppressing, denying them the right to resurface. Really, I refused to sleep, terrified that the dream world would imprison me in the same dullness and pessimism that had taken over my daily life. It might sound odd to others, but this is how badly I wanted to rid myself of a tasteless life. To feel bored when I'm both awake *and* asleep really terrifies me.

Then again, these are the kinds of thoughts that I tend to have at four o'clock in the morning, so a midday nap might not be so bad.

If I am to remain honest, I should say that there were some nights when I was feeling better. Perhaps I spoke with my friend that day, or I went on a really beautiful bike ride — whatever the reason, there were good days, too. On those evenings, I would think of the other possibility — the chance that I might stumble equally into some wondrous dream rather than a nightmare. A dream full of adventures and intense feelings. I would even welcome a hint of wildness, like a complicated fantasy story or a thrilling mystery, just to taste something a little different. On those nights, I would risk falling asleep.

Leaning my head against the window, I drifted, whether I wanted to or not. I dreamt of an apartment in Toronto. A cold place, industrial-looking with one huge and blindingly bright window set along a concrete wall. It looked like some kind of abandoned half-constructed flat. An upholstered couch, smoke-coloured, and a coffee table sat in the middle, both covered by a dusty plastic sheet. Only a single nazar boncuk hung on the wall, carrying the heavy responsibility of protecting the whole place. In the far corner, there was a treadmill and some flattened cardboard boxes. No artwork, no books, no rugs, no kitchen — the flat had none of the things that I loved the most.

In my dream, a close friend dropped by to invite me out for lunch at a new restaurant downtown. I couldn't tell you who it was or what she looked like, but I knew that I liked her. She waited patiently for me to finish folding my laundry, leaning on the doorjamb and watching me. I asked her about her day. She didn't even check her watch, but I could tell she was getting increasingly restless — she kept shifting positions, stealing glances toward the front door, sighing gently. After what felt like a long time, I finished folding my clothes. I picked up the laundry basket and tried to move past her, attempting to reach the bedroom beyond to put the clothes away. My friend didn't budge from the doorway.

"Is there something else that needs to be done?" she asked. "I can help you, and we can finish faster. I'm worried that the restaurant will be too crowded if we leave any later."

"You go on without me," I replied with indifference.

"What do you mean?" she asked. "I thought you were excited to try the place out?"

"I don't think I can go today."

Her eyebrows knitted together. "You can't even step away for lunch?"

I repeated myself, feeling exasperated. "You can go. It's fine."

"Did I do something to upset you?" she pressed. Her voice sounded strained.

"No, that's not it," I said. "I just can't hang out today, and I don't want you to miss out, so just go without me."

Clearly upset and eager to leave, my friend stomped to the front door and put her boots on. She muttered under her breath, "I don't fucking get you. I just watched you fold laundry for half an hour." She spoke angrily, making sure I would hear. "What do you possibly have to do today that you would refuse lunch with your friend?"

As if the answer was obvious, I replied, "I still have to walk on the treadmill."

In the dream, I had little time to accomplish all that I wanted, yet I still moved slowly. I wasn't relaxed, but I was unhurried. Sluggishly going from one task to the next, I knew that the walk on the treadmill would be leisurely, too, but it had to be done. I could not leave a task outstanding — it would make the completion of the rest of my to-do list futile. I would sooner implode.

She slammed the door behind her, and I jolted awake, startling the young woman seated next to me. The bus was still en route, driving smoothly along the shoreline. I had been asleep for barely five minutes. Looking out the window, I watched the waves of the Bosphorus crash against the empty sidewalk. The sun was beating down on the concrete, drying the wet edges of the pier before another wave hit.

I thought about the treadmill. Why did I dream of walking on a treadmill of all things? In the real world, I definitely would have chosen to go for a meal with my friend. More than that, I hate treadmills. I hate their rhythmic pace, the dizziness that comes with moving in place, their constricting space — and yet, the treadmill seemed so important to me in my dream. I absolutely had to walk on it, and it seemed like refusing to walk on it would unleash chaos onto the world. But at what cost? I knew it was just my imagination, but the thought of me enjoying a treadmill made me uncomfortable. It started creeping under the floorboards of my mind, like an insect looking to nest. My chest tightening, I felt lightheaded at the thought of doing a steady and almost hypnotic activity, and my face flushed with heat and panic. I desperately wanted to jump into the crashing Bosphorus waves.

My mother was the type of person to worry about such things. Simple, everyday stresses would unnecessarily steal all her energy. If a guest was coming over, she would start cooking two days before. She would make food that she knew her guests would love, and if she had to, she would drive to five different stores across the region to get the ingredients she needed. She would spend most of the day cleaning parts of the house that no one would see. Drenched in sweat, she would be hoarse from nagging us about how we should do better to keep the house cleaner. She was always the last to shower and would do so right before the guests arrived. We knew, of course, that the guests would come late. No one ever came on time, because that's how Turks always behaved. Still, she would scramble until the last second, just like they do on those competitive cooking shows. When the guests finally came and overwhelmed my mother with praise about her food, the décor, her well-mannered children, she would smile and humbly cast her eyes down. She would thank them with an "Ayağınıza sağlık" and tell them that she did nothing to deserve such compliments.

Naturally, after all her efforts, when the guests finally left, the exhaustion would hit her all at once, leaving her joints aching. She would have trouble getting up from the couch for a couple of days. My mother practically relished in the intense preparations and would invite people over every few weekends. It was a small thing to many, perhaps a forgettable Saturday in comparison to all the days that we live in our lives, but for her it was everything. She wanted people to be together, to laugh and share stories. Whether it was gossip or politics, the conversation never ceased at her dinner parties, and she loved that. She organized her personal calendar according to when our next guest was booked. It was the biggest disappointment for her to have to cancel an evening with friends. She would mope around and complain about it all day, as if she had hoped that her wrists would break while scrubbing the bathtub clean. She loved her dinner parties — I have attended hundreds of them. I gladly admit that I've inherited her propensity for entertaining.

So, why the treadmill of all things? I felt as if my mind was conspiring against my soul, my thoughts attacking me all at once. I wished that I hadn't fallen asleep. In the dream, I chose order, stability, routine, everything that I have grown to hate. The dullness of this life was starting to infect me on the inside, and I knew that I had to fix it before this dullness became irreversible. I was seeing the world in grey, and I knew there was so much more colour to it. Maybe it was my lively memories that were the real dream. Before I could stop it, my eyes felt weighed down and I closed them once again.

• • •

I was not in the apartment now. In this new dream, I was in someone else's dimly lit office. It felt cozy. Opposite a desk and filing cabinets were a couch with pillows, a fuzzy IKEA rug, a table with self-help books, and some fake plants. I was seated on the sunken leather couch with a tissue box in my lap. A woman with silver hair was seated across from me in a comfy chair, a notepad and pen in hand. The blinds were drawn.

She spoke gently, "Please continue, I think you were about to make a great point."

"I feel like I keep repeating myself," I replied quietly.

"I don't see it that way. It seems like you are taking several different approaches to try and understand the same issue as fully as you can. One of those pathways will be helpful, so please, keep trying. Tell me again how the loneliness makes you feel."

Ah yes, loneliness; the longest relationship I've ever had. Loneliness, you have returned to the conversation, though I feel like you never really left. Don't you think it's time for you to go finally? Move on. You've overstayed your welcome.

"Start anywhere," said the therapist. "I want to figure this out with you."

I took a deep breath. "My heart hurts," I said. The therapist nodded, and I continued. "I feel like I've been calling out this whole time. Loud and clear. Always the one to communicate first, making all the sacrifices. Bringing myself to others, forcing myself to make an effort, contributing to relationships, taking initiative in forging those connections. Still, nothing. I'm ready to give up now."

"Do you think people feel lonely around you?"

"I really hope not. I try to be present, to really hear people and be there for them."

"But you feel lonely around them, correct?"

"Yes, almost always."

"I'm following you. So, you're ready to give up. Why now?" she asked.

"Because I'm done trying." I sounded exasperated. "What more can I do? No one has been listening. No one is coming. I accept it now. There is no use screaming if it's just going into the void. My heart accepts that it will always be lonely. Maybe I can finally rest, knowing now that there is nothing more to be done. I've tried. I'm thinking that I could get used to the pain, that loneliness might become quieter if I accept that it's staying with me."

"That sounds difficult to experience so frequently."

"Exactly. I'm done." I tossed the tissue box onto the small table.

"Why do you feel like those connections that you've already made are not enough?"

"What do you mean?"

"You have connections," she said. "You have friends, family, people that you enjoy spending time with, right? Do you feel lonely around them?"

Embarrassed, I felt tears welling up. "I'm being selfish, aren't I?" I told her. "I should be grateful for those that I have."

"Hold on," the therapist insisted. "It is not selfish for you to want genuine connection. Humanity succeeds thanks to community. People depend on each other, which is the way it has always been. It is a fundamental human right to be wanted, to be heard, to have honest, trusting relationships — to be a part of a community."

I let that one sink in. Felt my throat tightening. Why couldn't I have what was meant to be mine? She said it was a human right to have trusting and fulfilling relationships, and yet, I was continuously denied.

"I am not saying your connections — your relationships and community — are bad," the therapist continued. "I'm asking you: What are they missing? Some part of you is not satisfied by those connections. I mean this in a non-condescending way, but what more do you need?"

"I — I'm not sure," I stammered.

"Ask yourself the question, 'What more do I need?' But not the person sitting in front of me on the couch. Ask the other one. The younger self, the Inner Child that's inside of you — ask them what they need."

I pondered the question for a moment. What does that kid need?

"To be understood?" I guessed, tears now gliding down my cheeks.

"Sounds like you're on to something. Why is that important to you?"

"I don't feel lonely around people who understand me," I replied. "People who don't question who I am as a person or make me feel like I need to be smaller. I like my own company. But most people make me feel lonely."

"How can you encourage or guide people to better understand you?"

"Um ..." I couldn't think of anything. My face was wet. I was already surrounded by bundles of used tissues.

"No, they can't do it," said the therapist in a kind manner. "The Inner Child can't answer that question very well; neither can the person in front of me, they are too busy crying. Ask the third one."

"Oh, ask the Higher Self, you mean?" I pulled three tissues and dried my tears.

"Notice how your body has been telling you something important," the therapist interjected. "Remember that tears fall for a reason. I explained to you before that they are indicators, and they each have names. What are *those* ones called?"

"Emotional pain." I spoke with confidence.

"Very good. Let's try to be more specific. Which feelings is the Inner Child experiencing when thinking about this subject?"

I thought for a moment. Looking inwards, I pictured my child self bawling their eyes out, huddled in the corner of a room. I bent down and placed a hand on their head. *What's wrong?* I asked. *Can I please help you?*

"I'm scared," I told the therapist. "Afraid that no one really knows me, that they won't want to know me. Afraid of the depth at which I feel emotions. I want to share that with others who don't understand it. I'm afraid of how well I understand other people and the world. That I'm too much for my friends and family, that I'm better off saving them the trouble of really knowing me."

"I want to make sure I understand you when you say you're too much. Do you feel very different from other people?" asked the therapist.

"Not *that* different," I replied. "But I feel like people make the decision for me. They put me to the side, not knowing where I belong. I am not their problem, not their responsibility, so it is easier for them to keep me at a distance. They admire my qualities and use me only when I am needed, then they abandon the rest of me. I didn't ask for this treatment. I didn't ask for my mind, my view of the world, and I definitely didn't ask for this separation from society. They place me far away, and it's so lonely. The effort needed to get to know me is too great for most people, I think."

"For the record, your intelligence and intuition are rare, and they are to be admired." The therapist spoke resolutely. "Each person is incredible in their own way, and I mean it when I say that it is a pleasure to hear your thoughts. I aim to help you see your greatest qualities in a more positive light one day."

I nodded, blushing at her response.

"We'll get to it, but probably not today," she said, scribbling down some notes. "Any other emotions related to your fear?"

The response came easily, like a dam being broken. "Disappointed and frustrated that I have to experience this pain and that I have to feel it all the time," I continued. "Guilty that I can't hide my pain anymore. Angry that I'm always the one working on myself, when other people could try harder to meet me halfway. Confused, because I feel like I'm not asking for a lot here. Why is it so hard for people? I'm just looking to be understood and accepted."

"Do you think that your Inner Child can handle feeling all of that?"

"It would be a lot for a child, I think."

She nodded. "I agree. So, we're not going to let the Inner Child defend itself in this situation. They're still learning — they are not fully equipped yet for these overwhelming feelings. The person in front of me is the one actually experiencing them, so they are in the thick of it, too. They can't help right now. It's the Higher Self who will be the guardian. They have the knowledge, the skills, the tools to take on this challenge. The Higher Self defends us best. They protect the happiness within when it is under threat. Lean on the Higher Self. Let the warrior handle it."

I nodded.

"Go for it," she said. "To not feel lonely, you said that you need to feel understood. How can you guide people to better understand you?"

I conjured up a familiar version of myself that was only a silhouette, but they were clearly me. They had this strong, untouchable aura. They moved so confidently, striding toward me, a glow around them. They placed a firm and warm hand on my shoulder.

"Stay open," I began. The therapist nodded in encouragement. "I am worthy just as I am. And show more compassion? I can work on trusting others to get to know me."

"A good first step. This is excellent progress." The therapist smiled. "I have more strategies for you around loneliness, but we'll have to save it for the next session."

Just as I looked to the wall clock by the desk, I heard an electronic chime *DING-ding* on the hour. I opened my eyes as the bus was stopping to let off passengers. My jaw was stiff and sore from being clenched.

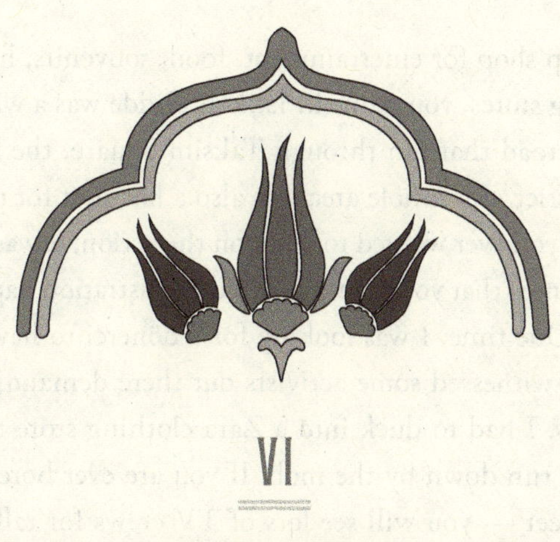

VI

BEYOĞLU

Rubbing the sleep from my eyes, I squeezed past the standing passengers and exited the bus. Heat blasted in my face immediately — the sun was showing no mercy today. Following the cobblestone alleyways, I passed several Haussmann-style buildings that reminded me of Paris, which were no doubt boiling inside in the hot Near Eastern summer. Weaving through narrow streets, I soon found myself in the famous district of Beyoğlu.

Known as a place of youthful energy, Beyoğlu had the latest in all aspects of the arts. Tourists loved the district as a one-stop shop for entertainment, food, souvenirs, high-end clothing stores, you name it. İstiklal Cadde was a wide pedestrian road that ran through Taksim Square, the heart of the district. The whole area was also a hot spot for protests. In case you ever wanted to be in on the action, it was almost a guarantee that you would find a demonstration happening there. One time, I was looking for a dönerci to have lunch when I witnessed some activists out there demanding new reforms. I had to duck into a Zara clothing store to avoid getting run down by the mob. If you are ever bored, walk this street — you will see lots of TV crews for talk shows and trivia quiz shows out testing the intelligence of the local population. If you're looking for attention without asking for it, you could always join the fashionably dressed people who spend hours at a café patio with their laptops. Needless to say, this place is never not busy.

It is understandable that people lose track of time here. To be clear, my goal was to walk through the district, and I was not going to buy anything. Especially since the last time I walked through Beyoğlu, I left with four shopping bags full of items without intending to shop at all. Keeping my eyes trained on the streetcar tracks at my feet, I strode down the road. The sun was setting my skin ablaze, and yet I didn't care to roll down the scrunched sleeves of my T-shirt. My fair shoulders might benefit from a little scorching, like the eel atop nigiri.

After passing store after store, café, restaurant, bar, karaoke bar, ten different kinds of banks, the new art museum, and the old art museum, the sudden scent of roasting chestnuts blinded me to everything else. That sweet and nutty aroma filled my nose. It didn't matter that I wasn't hungry; I had to grab a bag. Türkiye had some of the best street food available, and those delicious roasted chestnuts were calling to me. They were made perfectly every time. This particular vendor also looked fun to talk to — he seemed jolly and had a booming laugh, and large groups of tourists were smiling and waving back at him as they left his stall. I approached the jewels that were roasting on the food cart.

"Chestnuts for you?" he asked in broken but enthusiastic English.

"Türküm," I said with a half smile.

He switched to Turkish without hesitation, replying in the same playful tone. "Me too, but the question still applies! You want to buy some chestnuts? You look like someone who would appreciate a few roasted chestnuts. One bag, two?"

I couldn't hold in my giggles. "One bag!" I proclaimed.

He stuffed a paper bag to the top with freshly roasted chestnuts. I handed him the cash, though I felt like I should pay him more for the blessings that I just received.

"That smell!" I said, practically hypnotized.

"It smells like this life is worth living, right?" the vendor exclaimed, and I nodded vigorously in agreement. "I knew you'd get it. Enjoy, enjoy."

I gave a quick nod goodbye and turned to walk away, but he called out to me again. "Are you also going to leave me behind?" he shouted pitifully.

My stomach turned a little. It was something about the way he implied that I was abandoning him. I turned to face him again, confused.

"Every day I meet interesting people, but all they do is buy chestnuts," he whined. "Then they leave me. Why don't you stay for a little bit, my *obviously* Turkish friend? Tell me, how is life going? Can I please go with you sometimes?" He winked at me, maintaining his good humour.

Feeling a little shy, I mentally agreed to stick around for a few minutes to entertain him. I decided on the only topic that was occupying my mind. "I absolutely love chestnuts. No matter the season," I said honestly.

"Well, I have a lot of love to give. Do you need some more?" He smirked cheekily. "Two bags? Three? Take them home to your family!"

I shook my head, cracking a chestnut open. "You're a bad influence," I joked. "If I stay around you, I will clean out your whole stock."

"Oh, how kind. I can *almost* feel your passion! If only you would *really* buy me out, then I would truly feel like I'm loved." He offered a mischievous side-eye. "What is a local doing among the tourists at this busy time of day anyway? I am flattered if you are here only for a bag of İstanbul's most delicious snack."

I took a moment to reflect, not sure about how honest I should be with a random chestnut seller. "I've been away for a little while," I said. "I wanted to see how the city was doing."

"My friend, İstanbul is the same as it's always been." He patted my shoulder with a heavy, reassuring palm. "Nothing has really changed. Unless, of course, you've noticed something that I haven't? Sometimes the crab doesn't know it's boiling to death in the pot until it's too late! Tell me quickly!"

I examined the contents of the paper bag. "It does seem like İstanbul looks and breathes the same, but somehow it doesn't feel the same."

"Then you are the one who has changed." He gave me a wide smile. "That's a good thing, my friend! Why are you frowning? You have chestnuts in your hands. Everyone knows it's sacrilegious to frown when eating chestnuts."

"Is it? Is it a good thing that I've changed?" I asked, still staring into the paper bag.

"You don't think so?"

I looked up to see him still smiling, but with his eyebrows furrowed. I spoke quickly, suddenly aware that I didn't have to confess anything to this merchant.

"Sorry, I'm sure you want to get to the other customers."

I turned to leave a second time. He clasped his big hand on my shoulder again, but this time it felt welded down. He looked at me thoughtfully.

"My friend," he began. "I am not Nâzım Hikmet, so I don't have the best way with words, but I have a question for you. Why did you come back? I know it sounds blunt, but I am curious now. You said you were away for a while. I'm sure you had a good reason to go. Maybe you had a *really* good reason to stay over there, too, wherever you went. Unless you found an *even better* reason to come back? So, why are you here? Tell me your story, my interesting Turkish friend."

I wasn't sure how to offer a clear answer, because it was a thought that I was struggling with myself. I attempted a response.

"I had a great life here," I told him. "I loved everything about İstanbul, and I miss that feeling. These days, I'm having a hard time finding that spirited feeling again. I wondered if I might stumble upon it somewhere in the city."

He shuffled around the roasting chestnuts with his tongs. For a moment, I thought he hadn't heard me. When he finally spoke, his words were gentle.

"Sometimes we just need our origins, you know? It's like coming to the surface to breathe. You can always adjust yourself to another place, compromise, assimilate, but it will feel like putting on a mask. Wearing a mask for a long time doesn't feel good, you know? Rahatsız eder. At least, that's how I felt when I studied in America for a year."

He waved his tongs at me. "Don't tease me, but back when I was in school, I was top of my class in English. Despite my absolute *mastery* of the English language, America was not for me. It was the little things that I just couldn't get used to over there. To get along with others and fit in, I couldn't be my usual Anatolian Emre, I had to be this version called Californian Emre. It felt ridiculous. What a stupid mask that was. Maybe I don't know your whole story, my friend, but this one sounds kind of easy. I think you probably missed İstanbul because it let you live without that mask. You miss being yourself, no? Am I wrong?"

Emre's kind eyes made his serious question sound less forward. This random middle-aged Turkish man was speaking to me like he was my big brother, and I didn't know how to respond.

The lines around Emre's eyes crinkled as he watched me. He laughed.

"Yes, yes, I know I shine brightly, but don't stare at me!" He said it dramatically, as if rehearsing a line from a play. "I'm afraid I'll start to lose my brilliance in your eyes, and then I'll have to try harder to shine again!"

I let out a laugh. "I thought you weren't a poet," I said, and Emre bellowed again. "Thank you for your words. I needed to hear them."

He leaned in, voice low but still playful. "I know I'm just another amca, but we vendors, we like it when someone needs us," he admitted. "Some people search the alleyways of the city to find us, so we try to be someplace useful and soothe the souls of others, even if it's just through your stomachs." He turned to toss the chestnuts again, grinning to himself.

"Thank you, Emre Bay," I said and gave him a final nod. "I have stolen enough of your wisdom, I think."

"Nonsense, wisdom is to be shared. I thank you for hearing my thoughts, too. It frustrates me greatly when someone doesn't let me join the conversation, especially after I so intently listened to them. Those people are no friends of mine and certainly don't deserve these treasures!" He snapped his tongs at the chestnuts.

"I hope you make a good profit today," I said and turned to leave for a third time.

"Güle güle, my friend! I'll see you tomorrow for that second bag of chestnuts." Emre waved back, adding a friendly wink.

I'd devoured the rest of my snack before I reached the end of the street. I didn't stop — with each step I thought back to what he'd said about cultural assimilation. He'd had a good point. Had I just been wearing a mask for so long that I had forgotten who I was? Coming back to İstanbul, was I just trying to live as my old self again? But that thought didn't sit comfortably in my mind. When I was in Canada, I was privileged enough to still be myself. Not entirely, mind you, because there are some things that don't fit outside their context. Still, I wouldn't say that I was wearing a mask the whole time that I lived in Toronto. Both places were the two pillars of my identity. I never felt wronged by my time in Toronto, and not in İstanbul, either. No, there had to be more to that story. The vendor's words might have been partially true, but I knew my investigation had to continue.

VII

GALATA

The line to get into the tower was long, as always, but I had enough time on my hands to wait it out. A few British tourists ahead of me were snickering at the English translations of the historic panels that lined the walls. Reading aloud the panel about the Genoese reconstruction, the tourists pointed out amusing spelling mistakes in the sentences. They were reading about how Galata was a watchtower that looked out over the city to spot fires and approaching enemies. It reminded them of the first *Assassin's Creed* video game and how the main character jumped off the top of the tower to land impossibly in a pile of hay. I didn't tell them that the game was one of my favourites. When I played it, I used to ignore all my character's missions and would instead climb to the tops of old buildings, just so that I could admire the views of the city. The game's developers had envisioned old İstanbul beautifully. The sepia colours and the haziness of the scenes were pretty accurate to the actual feeling of being at the top of the tower in the summertime. Whenever the afternoon sun overtook the skies on a humid day, the city turned a mix of soft burnt sienna and yellow ochre, the warm air smelling like that addictingly sweet cigarette smoke that I had inhaled back at the airport terminal.

When it was finally my turn, I took the elevator up several floors and then walked the last two flights to the tower's observation deck. Stepping out onto the balcony, the scene felt so familiar to me. My silhouette added to İstanbul's skyline as I peered out onto the city and the Galata Bridge below. It looked as if toy cars were flooding the roads, with people hurrying along like a horde of red ants. The honking horns and shouts of fishermen sounded so far away. The tower was not too tall, but it was high enough for you to want to grip your phone a little tighter when taking a panoramic shot. I noticed again that the city was adorned with new buildings, mostly glass and steel skyscrapers, all rising high above Galata Tower. Once the tallest point in the city, the tower was now in the shadows of countless metallic structures. I felt a little resentful toward this change. Even though Toronto had also changed a lot over the years, its changes weren't as jarring as İstanbul's transition to its contemporary self. Toronto already had its rectangular buildings that naturally got taller as the population grew, and then the city expanded farther into the surrounding green fields. Contrary to this, İstanbul had ancient bones. Its aged magnificence was slowly being replaced with metal limbs, the city becoming more and more like a bionic body.

The İstanbul from my childhood was disappearing, being erased by urban development. Nevertheless, I took comfort in seeing the historic monuments of my youth still standing. They acted as landmarks in the skyline, orienting my place in the city. For that reason, the view was still breathtaking.

Clutching the railing, I noticed the concrete border was entirely covered in graffiti. My sister and I had once carved our names into the wood railing, many years earlier, but they had since been covered up by concrete and other names. I carefully combed through the many declarations of love and name tagging, trying to find one that I recognized, making a little game out of it. Eyes glued to the border, I did two full circles around the observation deck and gave up halfway through the third round. *Boş ver*, I thought to myself.

A young tourist with reddish hair and looking a little lost was trying to figure out how to use the coin-operated tower viewers. He was a boy of no more than sixteen and was standing apart from his school group, all of them huddled inside and shielding themselves from the sun. Each was wearing a light blue T-shirt with a treble clef illustrated on the front and the name École Secondaire Catholique de Sainte-Anne printed on it. My best guess was that it was a Catholic high school orchestra band on an international field trip. A wave of nostalgia swept over me.

Those were the days! I wasn't in band, though I was a visual arts student at our high school. We had our own European trip, though I really only remember the amazing lunch served to us by an old lady in Assisi during a pit stop on our way to Rome. Even then, I knew how lucky we were to be able to travel with our school. I remembered rolling my eyes at classmates who complained that the leisure time was too short or that the bus rides were too long. I thought them to be ungrateful. I remembered thinking, *There are homeless women begging on the side of the road to feed their sons, but no,* you *don't think about them. You're going to continue complaining that your fast-food pizza place is better than the two-hundred-year-old family-run restaurant in Florence? How spoiled.* Maybe I was being too hard on them. After all, we were teenagers. But despite being the same age as them, I couldn't help but feel that most of my classmates never understood the privileges that we had been given. It could be because I grew up within an immigrant family and had learned early on that hard work could get you a lot of nice things in life, while luxury was rare. I had always recognized good fortune when it was given to me, because it dazzled and had a certain forbidden air about it. I knew it shouldn't be within my grasp, so I should hold on tight if I happened to come across it.

I kept running my hands over the engraved names, looking out over the Bosphorus and breathing deeply. I started to think that, maybe if I was lucky, I could fuse with the İstanbul air and just exist here as a floating breeze.

The boy with the reddish hair caught my attention again. He seemed exasperated by the tower viewer and yelled to his classmates for help.

"Venez! Aidez-moi!" he pleaded at the glass window.

His classmates were standing on the stairs, blocking people from going up or down between floors. They shook their heads, pointing to the glaring sun.

He huffed and turned to me. "Do you know this?" he asked, pointing to the machine.

"Oui, je peux vous aider," I replied.

"Ah! Vous parlez français?" he said, looking shocked.

"Oui, j'habite au Canada."

"Vraiment? J'ai cru que tu étais Turc. Mais attend, I am supposed to practise my English." He said the last part proudly, with a slight French accent. I raised an eyebrow at his sudden switch to informal French, but never mind, we were going to continue in English. I could let that little hint of rudeness slide.

"I am also Turkish," I assured him.

"I know it. It is *clear*," he said while gesturing his hand up and down my body.

Finally, someone said that I looked Turkish today, but it somehow felt like a backhanded compliment. I was curious what gave it away. Normally the roundness of my cheeks or the bushiness of my eyebrows might suggest Near Eastern origins, but only if people really pay attention.

"How did you know that I was Turkish?" I asked him.

He giggled and answered mockingly, "You look like this tower is your *home*. You live *here*," he said while showing me the ground of the observation deck. I didn't understand.

"I'm joking," he said. "But I know *for sure* you are *definitely not* European."

There it was. The mentioning of "otherness" could not go unnoticed. For those who've never experienced this, go take Edward Said's book *Orientalism* off the shelf. To put it very briefly, the text refers to the self-affirmations of European identity via criticism of Islamic civilizations. One of my favourite reads, I think Said's book explains best how Turks might never be considered as "Western" in the eyes of the West. At the same time, we do not comfortably fit into the "East" category, either, so we must accept putting a checkmark next to the "Other" category box. It's a fascinating conversation, one that expands beyond nationality. This boy, coming from a European perspective, instinctually recognized this complexity. Many people interact with me in this same way, making assumptions and passing judgment, mostly without a second thought. Whenever I was othered or questioned about my background, I would have a minor identity crisis. My responses were not convincing enough for people — I don't know why I always tried so hard to explain myself, to provide a definition of who I was.

Throughout my life, I have always heard "I don't know what you are, but I do know that you're not one of us." Sometimes, the person was referring to the way that I cooked food — too many spices to be considered European, not enough heat to be called Asian. I was always described as existing somewhere in the middle. Another time, a Canadian acquaintance wouldn't let me join their BIPOC group because my skin was too light for his narrow definition of BIPOC. To which I responded, "Where do you categorize people who celebrate Ramadan and pray in mosques, who live in Asia, and whose family grew up that way for hundreds of generations? Where do I fit, on your BIPOC scale?" He never answered me, but I saw him practically implode in front of my eyes.

Most of the time, people have othered me after hearing me speak. For some reason, my words seemed to confuse people. I speak confidently in English, with very rare interruptions of a Turkish accent; however, the way that I speak is very close to Arabic. My expressions are poetic and illustrative. Many have compared my speaking to that of eloquent philosophers, but really, they meant that they didn't quite follow what I was saying. Or, more accurately, that people never thought of expressing a sentence in that way. This mix of fluent English with Middle Eastern angles — it was rare for most people to hear. As if watching me add grated garlic to plain yogurt, they did not understand it. They questioned my inner balance. I always felt a little proud of that. Of course, it was hurtful when people denied me my identity, not knowing how I fit in to their own categories. It has happened often enough. Either way, I try to show patience and understanding when people are working to decipher if I'm East or West. I'm thinking that these naïve people are coming across the "Other" category for the first time. I see how "Other" could be ominous and fearful to them because of its vagueness. But for many of us, it gives us room to breathe. A space where we can remain authentic to ourselves, without the confines of a label. East or West? I don't know. Can't I be everything? Can't I be nothing? Why are the options so limiting? Why can't this be a fill-in-the-blank form, rather than multiple choice? Why do I sometimes look Turkish and sometimes don't?

"You look sad?" the boy interjected suddenly.

"No, sorry, I was thinking about something else," I said, trying to collect myself. "Um, this machine needs two liras, not one." I showed him the worn-out sticker instructions on the side.

"Wow, you said 'sorry' like a real Canadian, I have to tell my friends." He smirked at me and leaned an arm on the machine.

This kid. First it was the informal French, then the otherness, and now the Canadian stereotyping. He's got some nerve.

"You need *two* liras," I repeated, failing to sound polite.

"I do not have two liras!" He sighed loudly and threw his head back. "I already put in one lira ..."

I fished a spare lira from my pocket while he was pouting and put it in the slot. "Have fun," I said before turning away.

"Generous," he replied, trying to sound surprised, but it was obviously fake. He seemed pleased with himself as he looked through the binoculars greedily, turning the machine left, then right, exploring the skyline.

I didn't take even five steps toward another part of the observation deck before he called out to me again: "Étranger!"

Just like that, one of my favourite books came to mind. I know the boy meant nothing by it, but I recalled the text by Albert Camus, a reading from my French class in high school. In the book *L'Étranger*, the main character, Meursault, talked about existentialism in an almost lyrical way, which I kind of loved. If anyone could understand my ongoing identity crisis, my indifference with life, it would probably be Meursault. How telling that my mind immediately thought of that book when I was in İstanbul searching for my missing passion for life.

"Thank you for your help," the boy said with a wave. I nodded.

After only a few seconds spent admiring the sights, a girl wearing the same blue T-shirt peeked her head out of the doorway and called out to her classmate.

"Renard! On y va," she insisted, and then gestured for him to come inside.

They engaged in a short debate, Renard trying to buy more time to keep looking through the tower viewer, while the girl claimed that the tour bus was going to leave without him.

Their group left, and I headed inside shortly after. Walking through the restaurant to the elevator, I recalled attending a dinner at Galata Tower when I was ten years old. My uncle had bought the family tickets to a belly dancing performance with a fancy dinner included. Nergiz and my cousin were even invited to dance on stage, a fun little routine before dessert. I had a good time. The music and crowd were so lively. The sounds of the traditional instruments were enchanting. It was hard not to enjoy yourself in such a setting.

Now that I was thinking about it, like my unappreciative classmates from long ago, wasn't I being selfish, too? Wasn't wanting more out of life something that a selfish person would say? The thought had crossed my mind many times today, but something still wasn't fitting quite right. I have been told that I deserved better, that my time would come, that I was allowed to want abundance. Was that why my current life didn't feel good enough, because I lacked that fun side, the self-fulfilling joys? Did I truly deserve more, or were those just pretty words meant to keep me around?

Maybe the reason I have been called a philosopher is because I ask too many questions about how to live life. Very few people seem interested in exploring such things with me. "Just live life!" they have said to me. Well, that's what I thought I was doing, but somehow, I think I have been doing it wrong.

The heat was starting to get to my head — all at once everything looked too shiny with the sun's reflections. I made my way down the winding stone staircase back to the main floor. I braced myself, trying to build the courage needed to navigate through the horde of pedestrians that filled the streets. I didn't like being among so many people — there were too many chances to get robbed or be yelled at for simply looking at someone the wrong way. In most places, tempers tend to run especially hot on warmer days. Alas, the city was too densely populated — people and their bad attitudes were unavoidable.

So, dodging shoulders and slipping between gaps in the crowd, I made my way out and started toward one of the most congested places in İstanbul.

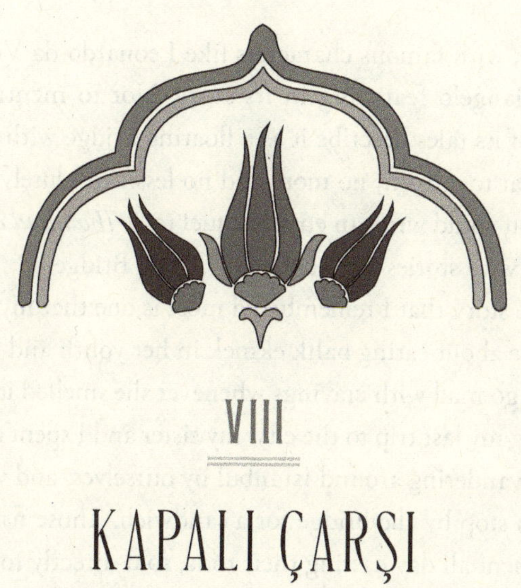

VIII

KAPALI ÇARŞI

Leaving Karaköy quarter behind, I started crossing the Galata Bridge, which was lined with highly focused middle-aged fishermen, and strode purposefully toward the Eminönü district. The bridge has remained iconic throughout Turkish history. Some might say it's a critical point in İstanbul's interconnectedness. My father had told me the history of every little corner of İstanbul, and Galata was often a recurring character. The larger suspension bridges that crossed the Bosphorus tended to get a lot of attention from foreigners, but the Galata Bridge has a particularly fun history, with famous characters like Leonardo da Vinci and Michelangelo featuring in its story. Not to mention that some of its tales describe it as a floating bridge with a toll of one goat to cross it, no more and no less. Absolutely legendary. You could write an entire sequel to *A Thousand and One Nights* with stories just about the Galata Bridge.

The story that I remembered most is one that my mother told me about eating balık ekmek in her youth and how she would go mad with cravings whenever she smelled it nearby. During my last trip to the city, my sister and I spent an afternoon wandering around İstanbul by ourselves, and we made sure to stop by the bridge for a sandwich. Those fishermen, who spent all day casting their rods, sold directly to the restaurants and food stalls that lined the bottom half of the bridge. The freshly fried mackerel was salty and crispy, the white bread fluffy and warm. Maybe it was because we were exhausted from walking for hours, or it could have been because we're our mother's children, but my sister and I agreed that those sandwiches were some of the best we had ever eaten. Crossing the water now, I resisted stopping at the stall to pick up a portion for myself to snack on. Those chestnuts were still sitting in my stomach, and no amount of walking was helping me digest them.

After almost an hour spent enjoying various food smells and strolling by the water, my eyes had started to glaze over. I hadn't realized that I'd weaved through several walkways and eventually stumbled upon Zincirli Han. In the Fatih district of İstanbul, my body was quickly searched by security personnel at a tucked away part of Kapalı Çarşı. Passing under the dimly lit archway, I entered into a hallway of gold and silver chains of every grade and swept my eyes over a covered street full of jewellery stores that left me stunned. Kapalı Çarşı is a huge market that spans blocks, rivalling modern shopping malls in size. Like much of İstanbul, the market has been rebuilt numerous times in response to fires and earthquakes, especially after the Siege of Constantinople, but much of its early architecture is still in its bones. I became giddy remembering the Halıcılar Caddesi, not too far from where I entered, and nearly skipped past the diamonds to get to the rugs.

Gorgeous Turkish rugs spilled out of every doorway on the covered street. Threads of deep garnet, soft olive green, striking indigo, fading stormy blue … Under the gentle lamppost lights, the rugs' intricate patterns and shining fabric were a feast for the eyes. I wanted to cover myself in them, or at least sink into a pile of rugs and stay there for a good while. I'm sure no one would judge me — the merchants knew that feeling, too. Nothing gave me a stronger sense of nostalgia than seeing a Turkish rug. Whenever I saw a towel or a doormat labelled "Made in Türkiye" while shopping in Canada, a great sense of pride welled in me, followed by an emptiness in my chest. No matter how excited I get to see a little piece of home, it's never the same when it is imported.

The stores that lined the bazaar filled me with such joy that I probably looked ready to burst. To see high quality Turkish goods sold in the Grand Bazaar itself, made by local artisans who were chatting over tea right in front of me, provided a feeling of elation that was truly irreplaceable. My cheeks hurt from smiling.

"Müşteri var," said a middle-aged woman in a sing-song voice from inside one of the store coves. She was alone in the room with rugs draped over every inch of the space. In front of her, layers and layers of rolled up and folded rugs served as temporary seating for customers. She was at a loom, her busy hands weaving the beginning of a greyish rug with ivory details. Her soft brown curls fell out of a ponytail, and her twinkling chocolate-coloured eyes peeked at me from under her blow-dried bangs. She looked like my beautiful and caring mother.

"Ellerinize sağlık," I said politely, trying not to disrupt her concentration. I gestured to the rug. "It's coming along beautifully."

"Thank you, my child." She spoke without taking her eyes off the loom. "Were you looking to buy something today, or are you only an admirer? I welcome both."

"Just admiring this time."

"Have a seat." She nodded her head toward the tiny plastic chair in front of her. "Tea or coffee?"

"No, thank you." I shook my head feverishly. "I've had both already."

"Tea doesn't count for Turkish people, it's like drinking water." She winked at me. "We drink it ten times a day, before and after every call to prayer." She called toward a back wall covered entirely in rugs, "Ömer! Emekli çay!"

The woman continued to work rhythmically and didn't look the least bit fazed by the heat. She was moving her arms nonstop, but there wasn't a single drop of sweat to be seen.

"Sorry," she began. "My husband is supposed to chat with the customers while I work, but he's rewatching sports highlights right now and can't multitask."

"It's not a problem," I assured her, staring at her hands. "Rugs tend to leave me mesmerized, so consider me entertained. I have such a fondness for them."

"Why does that sound a little dejected?" The woman kept her eyes on the loom, her mouth maintaining a small smile.

She gave off an air of comfort and warmth, so I decided to confess myself to yet another stranger today. "I don't live here anymore," I told her. "I haven't been back here in more than a decade, so I miss some of the little things about home, like the rugs."

"Hmm." Her smile faded. "I've made every single one of these rugs, and it hurts me to think that someone has made a place for a rug in their home but couldn't get their hands on one." She glanced toward the back wall, waiting for her husband to emerge.

"Don't mistake me, Usta," I rushed to add. "Pretty Turkish rugs are sold all over the world, but it's better when you can actually meet the artist herself. It feels different to buy a rug when you've had a chance to see someone make it in front of you — to see the skill and effort it takes, where the fabric lives, what the artist looks like."

"Ahh, so you're a romantic?" She laughed and switched coloured threads. "I'm joking, of course. I, too, understand the joys of a Turkish rug and how it makes my heart pound with pride to see one. I thank you for your high standards and for taking the time to drop by today." She winked at me a second time. "So, before you ran away from home, which district were you from?"

Cue the nosy Turkish auntie. "Beykoz," I replied swiftly.

A man with a slight belly slid past a rug on the back wall like he was opening a hidden door and briefly revealed a small back room with a TV tuned to a loud soccer game. He walked over to us, one light-coloured tea and one vişne juice on a circular wooden tray, which included a bronze plate filled with a tower of colourful Turkish delights.

Ömer's booming voice startled his wife. "Beykoz? You're Turkish? I've never seen a paler Turkish person in all my life!" His tone was friendly. He looked at me curiously as he placed the tray atop a small table, alongside scissors and threads.

"Yazıklar olsun," his wife said in a rising tone. Her smile was gone now, replaced with slightly gritted teeth and an accusatory gaze. "Do you want our customers to look like your aunt Serap? Should they wear a loose headscarf and spit out sunflower seeds while gossiping about how their neighbour always makes the baklava too dry? Would that be a more accurate depiction of Turkish people?"

She had stopped working the loom and slapped her lap with both hands in one snappish movement. Ömer listened to his wife intently.

She continued, "What about your cousin Hakan? Should our customers smell like old cigarettes and cough like they are about to lose a whole lung? Should they yell at the football players on TV, calling them 'actors' whenever they fall to the ground? Sound Turkish enough for you? Do you need more examples of proper Turkish people?"

She wasn't yelling at him, but her words cut like a chef's knife. The vein in her neck had swelled during her rant, but it relaxed when her eyes caught mine again. She mumbled to herself, "Allahallah!"

It was Ömer's turn to look chastised, but instead he smirked like a mischievous child.

"Okay, okay, fıstık. I didn't mean it as an insult. I'm genuinely interested in our young customer here." He said it more quietly than his naturally loud voice, giving the illusion that he was the calm one in the relationship.

He took a seat on the same pile of rugs as his wife, sitting very close to her, their thighs pushed together. He said to me, "You're not offended, right? Have some tea."

"It's quite all right," I said, and grabbed the watered-down tea. "I know that I'm a little paler than most, since I've been away for a while."

"Did you go to the dark side of the moon or what?" he joked, watching his wife to see if she'd let a laugh escape.

"Ömer." She elbowed him, but her pleasant expression reappeared. She kept her eyes on the threads.

"I was in Canada. They have long winters there, and so I lost some of my colour." I gestured to my face. I should charge people money for always asking me this question.

"Ah, I can tell — you have a subtle accent," Ömer said cheekily.

The weaver interrupted her husband with a whisper, but we were sitting so closely that I could still hear her. She spoke evenly, her tone threatening: "Allah akıl dağıtırken, sen kapının arkasında mı kaldın?"

The tea really did taste just like water. I downed the whole thing and placed the tulip-shaped glass back on the tray, and then popped an orange-flavoured Turkish delight into my mouth. I watched the weaver's husband for his reaction, but he looked like he was enjoying the verbal beating he was receiving from his wife. Eyes shining, he pushed her shoulder gently like a teasing classmate.

"Vayyy. Where did I find such a smart one? Why can't you share some of those brains with your husband, hmm?" Ömer replied.

I smiled awkwardly.

"You stare too much," she hurried to tell Ömer. "I can't focus."

Ömer was quicker. "It's not my fault. Allah gave you beauty, and I was given the eyes to admire it."

Why was I the one that was blushing?

"Ömer …" She sounded disappointed but failed to hide her growing grin.

"What? Incapable of retaliation, aşkım?" He chuckled and his whole belly shimmied, threatening to unbutton part of his perfectly ironed shirt. "Maybe I've finally found a way to tame this tigress." He beamed at me.

I turned my gaze to the loom and wondered if they would offer me another cup of tea or if I had to endure more of their flirty banter first.

"Hayatım," the weaver began coyly, "how dare you mistake me for a soul that could be tamed." Her eyes gleamed as she played along with her husband's games.

"Ohh." Ömer mimicked being shot in the heart. "Critical hit! She's not a tigress, she's a sniper. I could have used you during my military service."

"Everyone knows that the only useful thing you did during your service was to eat all the leftover food in record time. Even your superiors were amazed." She finished her glass of juice with a single swig.

"They liked me because I'm a funny guy," he said, still rubbing the invisible bullet wound.

I thought briefly about leaving, giving them some time alone to flirt in peace. The weaver interrupted my thoughts before I could take action.

"Maydonoz," she said to Ömer. "You're supposed to be engaging our customers in conversation and selling rugs, but instead you're playing with me and preventing me from completing my work. I'll go hungry at this rate. Not you, obviously, but I definitely will."

Still unfazed, Ömer whispered into his wife's ear, "So, you are aware that I was flirting?"

She stood up from her rug pile and took the tray with her. "Let me get you another glass of tea while my husband gathers his wits, since he can't seem to do so in my presence."

I nodded a quick thank-you and watched Ömer as he in turn watched his wife leave behind the rug-door again.

"Ateşli kadın," he said to me, as if I knew exactly what he was talking about. "She's like an ember, ready to become fire with the slightest breeze."

"It's a wonder — how can she make all of these stunning rugs when there's such a happy distraction hanging around her?"

Ömer watched the rug-door. "I do it on purpose."

"I'm sorry?"

"I distract her on purpose," he said more seriously. "She gets consumed by her craft and will go to bed with aching hands. She has arthritis now, you see. Not as young as she used to be, I know it's hard to believe by looking at her." He sighed and turned back to me. "She gets so caught up with making and selling rugs that she doesn't notice how it hurts her, so I try to force her to take breaks every now and then. It hurts me more to see her ache."

"Why does she keep going, if it hurts her so much?"

"That is her signature move — she shows people she cares by working herself to the bone. We don't need more rugs to sell, but she wants us to be financially secure. Not to mention, she enjoys the art — she always wants to make her art available to people who appreciate it. There's nothing I could say to stop her completely, nor do I want to. She deserves to be happy, every single day, and if she needs to keep making rugs to be happy, so be it. And if I need to give her hand massages every night to help the pain, or lovingly disrupt her work with forced breaks, then I will do it."

Ömer seemed calmer. He looked down at his intertwined fingers and smiled to himself.

"You love her very much," I stated. "Anyone can see it. I think you're the one that makes her happy, not the rugs."

"Don't let her hear you," he giggled. "'How dare you assume I would choose you over my rugs, Ömer!'" He imitated his wife's voice in a hushed tone.

The weaver re-emerged from behind the rug-door, with another cup of lightened tea and two glasses of juice this time.

Ömer spoke at a regular volume: "I'd like to think that the rugs and I are playing a friendly derbi — we're using each other for a greater cause," he explained.

"Kocam." The weaver handed her husband a cup of juice. "Drink this while I talk to our young friend here about rugs, which is what you should have been doing."

Ömer took the glass and sipped it obediently while watching his wife.

The weaver took up her chair but didn't engage with the loom. She grabbed her own cup of juice and gestured with her eyebrows, encouraging me to sip my tea.

"So, if I remember correctly," she paused and searched for an answer inside her glass. "You ran away to Canada, because ...?"

"I studied in Canada, then began to work there. It was a natural transition," I added.

"Because you went to school and started a career there, I see. Now you miss home and all the little things that remind you of home, so you came back. Is that about right?"

"I'm here temporarily," I corrected her. "I will go back to Canada in a few days."

"Why temporarily? Why not stay?" She was puzzled. "I thought you missed it here. Why not live in İstanbul for the long term?"

Ömer watched me silently as he snatched a yellow Turkish delight from the plate.

"I-I'm not sure," I stammered. "I don't really have a good enough reason to stay, I suppose? My entire career is in Toronto — how could I leave that behind? My friends are all over there. My … um —"

"I'm not convinced." The weaver spoke bluntly. "Your story is not some small pocketbook. Yours is an epic, I feel it. There's something more that you're not telling me."

"So much for talking about rugs …" Ömer chewed on his lemon-flavoured candy. The weaver gave him another elbow jab, but Ömer was quick to stabilize his half-drunk glass of juice.

This woman really did seem like my mother. An equal balance of eager to help and absolute nosiness about everything. She wanted to voice an opinion, but honestly, I didn't even know what problem she would be addressing. Who knows the true reason why I'd made the decisions that I had? Without really knowing me, could this auntie possibly know what was better for me?

"Fine," the weaver said. "Rugs it is." From under the loom, she picked up a rug about the size of a small pillowcase and handed it over to me. It had the same colour scheme as the large rug that she was weaving currently, but the designs were completely different.

"You see this one? This little rug that looks nothing like the one that I'm making right now?" she asked. I nodded. "They're different, but the same."

"Oh, I love her metaphors," Ömer said enthusiastically. He was met with an impatient glance, and he shut himself up with another sip of juice.

"I don't like to plan my final designs," the weaver began, holding up the smaller rug. "Because life never really follows a plan. You can prepare all you want, but there are always other forces at play, ones you could have never predicted. At least, that's how *I* feel about it. Others will disagree, naturally. This maquette is more like a brainstorming session."

I examined the modest rug. It had more geometric patterns than its parent rug and less floral detail. The colours were arranged in a gradient, a more gradual shift in tones than the striking contrast of shades on the larger rug.

"I improvise and learn as I go," the weaver said, gesturing to the large half-made rug still on the loom. "I try not to unravel my rugs, either. I feel like it defeats the purpose of learning, so I'm not one to erase the work that I've already done. I'm the only one who could even notice a mistake, because I'm the one who makes the design. To be frank, the plan is that there is no plan."

Ömer hummed and nodded in agreement.

"This larger rug was meant to look just like this maquette, but once I started the final version, I got more ambitious. I began to feel differently about the colours, and my hands wanted to weave the thread in another way. I didn't copy the example; I just allowed the threads to follow their own will."

I looked at the maquette again, gently gliding my fingertips over the myriad silk strands.

"The little rug was a summary of what I thought I wanted. Once I started my craft, I let the loom take me in a different direction. I soon realized that this new path suited me better. In a way, making this rug was an essential step so that I could figure out what I didn't want my larger rug to be."

Cradling the maquette in my hands, I thought about my own life. How my parents had planned out their immigration to Canada so that their children could live a life that was better than they had ever imagined for themselves. My education, my career, all growing from the same seed that my parents had planted. It was almost entirely planned out for me, and I never differed from that path — their ideas were valid, safe, comfortable. I saw what they were trying to do, and so I followed their plan. Still, seeing the larger rug take on such a beautiful form, I began to wonder if sticking to my plans was more harmful than helpful. Was I only doing what my family wished or expected of me, rather than what I wanted? I had never questioned it before.

"One last thought before you go, because I know a wandering mind when I see one," the weaver said. Both Ömer and I listened intently.

"Look at the back of this rug." The weaver pointed to the part of the loom that had been facing me the whole time. "Think about the difference between the front of a rug and the back — what people see versus what is hidden when the rug is placed on the floor or the wall."

I tried looking at the rug-in-progress with fresh eyes and then at the finished maquette in my hands.

"The back, the part that people don't see, the part that is important only to the artist and no one else, tells you a lot more about the rug than the front. The back is slightly more detailed. It has a clearer history of what happened when making the rug, and to me, it makes a lot more sense. To me, the back is more beautiful than the front."

Ömer rested his palm on his wife's back and gave it a gentle rub.

"In life, people will always judge us for the decisions that we make, because that's all they can see. They don't see our internal dialogue, our small battles or victories, our sleepless nights — they don't get to see any part of our journey. They see only the end result. They watch from the outside. They judge only what they can see, and they can only see the front of the rug."

I nodded. I was starting to understand where she was leading me.

"Balım, if you are in the middle of weaving a rug and you hate the design that you've created, just change the plan. When it comes to making your best rug, how you feel about your decisions is the only thing that truly matters."

"Hmm," I said aloud, reflecting on her words.

"No one understands your struggles better than you do, so I'm not going to pretend that I have all your answers. Stay in İstanbul or not — it's your decision. But I sincerely hope that you are not avoiding a major change in your life, like moving to a different city, because it would take you down a harder path. The rougher road might be the more fulfilling one."

My heart beat louder at her words. She made it sound so simple.

"Rugs don't make themselves, you know." The weaver's eyes glistened. "There are hard choices to make along the way. Just make sure they are choices that you really want to make."

Ömer applauded as if signalling the end of his wife's wisdom. The weaver tossed a green Turkish delight in her mouth. We stood up, and I glanced back toward the entryway to see the store had filled with another six customers. They were flipping over rugs and having hushed conversations about the quality and price.

"I'm sorry," I said quickly. "I hadn't realized that you had customers! I wouldn't have taken up so much of your time."

"Nonsense," Ömer assured me. "Ayaklarını sürttün. They arrived only a moment ago, and they're still perusing."

"I told you I welcome both buyers and admirers of rugs," the weaver said. "It was a pleasure having tea with you."

"The pleasure is mine," I emphasized. "My heartfelt thanks for offering me tea that I didn't know I needed."

The weaver winked. "I knew you'd get it."

IX

SULTANAHMET

As time settled into late afternoon, I passed a large fountain that sprayed cool water on my sunbeaten face. It was the final hours of a hot day, and calm evening air would soon fall over İstanbul. I admired the wildflowers and the colourful array of roses highlighted by the soft light. Sultanahmet Meydanı was a huge open park with stone pathways that filled the space between Sultan Ahmet and Ayasofya. Back when the city was still called Constantinople, this area was a hippodrome where thousands of spectators watched battles and races on a regular basis. It wasn't hard to imagine, given how much of İstanbul's original architecture remains. One could easily picture the park as an arena. Greek, Roman, Egyptian, German histories, you name it, there was still evidence of their presence all around the greenspace. That's one of the things that I liked about İstanbul — you could retrace someone's footprints so easily because they were still here. Strolling through the gardens, I passed families on summer outings and hordes of tourists. Each tourist I spotted took turns standing on top of a stone bench to get a good photo with the history that surrounded them.

Watching these photo-ops take place, I recalled a time when I was eight years old and sweating terribly at the nearby Gülhane Park. My sister and I were absolutely exasperated, tired of my father asking us to take picture after picture with his Nikon film camera. We complained nonstop, were caught sulking in every shot. We had just finished touring Topkapı Palace, and we were looking forward to the lahmacun and cola lunch that he had promised us. My mother had already run under the shade of a tree and begged us to smile for just one more photo so that we could hurry up and head into an air-conditioned restaurant to escape the heat. I vividly remembered a şerbetci walking by us then — he looked so unusual to me. My father's eyes lit up as if he'd spotted a shooting star, and he called the juice seller over. The şerbetci was wearing a thin white button-up shirt, a red vest with gold embroidery, matching shalwar pants, worn-down black leather shoes, and a plain red fez. He had a large stainless-steel pitcher strapped to his back, which had a long, skinny spout that curved up and over his shoulder. He also wore a type of makeshift belt that carried empty plastic cups and a compact change purse. I wondered how the seller wasn't boiling to death with all those clothes on in the middle of a hot summer's day. My father had asked the seller if he could purchase a cold drink from him, and he took out his wallet to pay for four cups. The seller winked at my sister and me and then poured a dramatic stream of limonata from the spout. My mother was quickly at our side, eager for her cup of the cold juice. My father finally managed to capture a photo of all three of us smiling as we held our juice, and the seller left to find his next customer. Looking around the square now, I couldn't spot a juice seller among the crowd, but I still found myself comforted by the phantom tartness of that chilled lemonade.

Clouds temporarily rolled over Sultanahmet Meydanı, dulling the cheerful colours of the garden beds and offering a break from the heat. I looked up at the clouds — it looked as if a brief summer rain shower might be coming. Looking toward the far side of the square, I searched for the street performers and buskers who were commonly found near the streetcar stop. On some days, they would draw large crowds; on others, no one would pay them any attention. Currently, a woman close to Ece's age was standing on a wooden crate reciting something and being completely ignored by every passerby. I sat down on a nearby bench and listened as she announced confidently that she was about to perform the final piece of her set. Her statement was met with applause from only two or three people.

In her ripped black jeans and white cotton T-shirt, she stared a hole into the backs of people's heads. Her voice rang out clear and firm, as if absolutely decided.

I hope you do not remember me.
Because if you remember *me*,
it would mean
I had a voice
that was merited
at a time of reckoning.
Because remembering *me*
in moments of thundering
would mean
I left a fierce impression
fighting in your memory.
And if there was indeed
a moment of darkness,
of rumbling, uneasiness,
then it is only natural
to seek the voices
that act as enlightenment.
But I hope you do not think of me.

For *I* wish to blend among history
as a person forgotten,
because that would mean
you did not *need* me.
I want my voice to be lost
among a thousand and one
delights in this world.
I beg for my voice to be swallowed
into that endless sky.
And I pray to all the forces
that you do not think of me.

Because if you *risk* thinking of me,
I will shine.
Moreso, my light will blind
like lightning striking,
the piercing burn of my fire
turned to stabbing blade.
You will fall at my feet
into the very mess you made.
I will be
ever-present
and unyielding.
I will be
precise
with my power.

The best among us
will be in awe
of my skill,
of my brilliance,
of my resilience.
I will take all
and show no mercy.
I will step up
and break all boundaries.

I *really* hope,
for *your* sake,
my name is not named.
Forget this, and do not call for me.
I said, do not ask for me.
For the love of Allah,
please
do not remember me.

The poet fell silent, standing still on that crate and staring into the horizon behind the crowd. The whole spoken word piece was full of crescendos and conviction. A few passers-by had turned back to look at her during the performance, only to be met by her glare. At the end of her monologue, like a doctor giving difficult news, she left us alone with our thoughts. Some people, myself including, came to our senses and clapped, but she had already stepped down off the crate, folded up her paper, and grabbed her bag to leave. Only she didn't leave but instead took a seat beside me on the bench, reaching into her bag for a steel water bottle and a nektarin.

I wrestled with whether or not to speak to her. I couldn't have done what she did — public speaking was too stressful. I settled on simply thanking her for the poem, since you never know when someone needs a little encouragement. Especially after an audience so lacking in enthusiasm. It was clear that she had spoken from a place of passion, putting her heart into her craft.

"Tebrik ederim," I said to the nectarine in her hand.

She ignored me and took another bite, the fruit crunching loudly.

"I enjoyed the poem," I added, trying to make eye contact. She kept eating her snack; I pressed on. "I was particularly impressed by your cadence. You spoke so well, like a politician giving a wartime speech."

She huffed at me, a smirk starting to form.

"Very original feedback. Did you even listen to my words, or are you just acknowledging that your hearing is working?" Her tone was quiet and condescending.

"I'm sorry?" I said, confused. "I didn't mean to offend you."

"I'm not offended," she said bitterly to her nectarine.

"You sounded a little angry just now."

"Well, can't I be angry? Aren't you angry, too?"

"Wait, what? Why would I be angry?"

"My poem? Did you not get it?" She rested the hand holding the fruit on her knee, searching my eyes for an answer.

"I'm sorry, I think I'm a little lost here."

"That much is clear," she returned, but less aggressively this time. She added, "Bekle," and got up to toss her nectarine in the nearby trashcan. When she sat down again, she took out a mini spray bottle of kolonya and offered me a spritz, which I automatically accepted. We both smelled like a freshly squeezed lemon.

"The poem," she continued harshly. "I said it means a lot to me, if you heard?" She didn't stop to hear my answer. "It's about my life here. The life of every young person. *Your* life. Aren't you tired of it being this way, too?"

I furrowed my eyebrows.

"Oh wait," she added, her tone shifting to something youthful and less patronizing. "Did I misunderstand? Are you not Turkish?"

"No, no, I am," I sighed.

"Okay, I wasn't sure." She looked me up and down. "You did say that you were lost before, and you have this mood about you, so I just assumed … I'm not sure."

"What mood?"

"I don't know, like you are trying hard to be here or to be acknowledged … Does that make any sense?"

"I'm sorry, I don't follow."

"Don't worry about it." She sounded tired. "It's hard for me to explain my intuitive nature to people, so just forget it."

She must have noticed my disappointment, because she added quickly, "I just observed that you were eager to talk to me about my poem, which is about something meaningful, which probably means that something meaningful has been on your mind lately, because you wanted to talk about it with someone. You used the poem as your excuse. That's all." She let out a full breath. "Forget it," she said with finality. "I think too much."

"No," I said gently. "You are completely right. This whole day I've been contemplative, self-reflective. You must have picked up on that."

"Right!" Her eyes lit up. "And what I was saying was starting to resonate with you? Maybe? No?"

"The poem definitely left an impact," I said honestly, still not sure if we were on the same page.

Despite being close to the waitress in age and sharing Ece's ability to speak her mind, the poet's disposition was very different. Though well spoken and thoughtful in her poetry, her in-person interactions were a little scattered. Contrary to her assertive poem, her conversation skills revealed self-doubt and wavering confidence. She couldn't settle between standing her ground on an opinion or being more accommodating to the views of others. She spoke quickly and would forget to breathe, like she had a mind that ran ahead of the rest of her. Still, she had this raw intelligence about her. Like how İstanbul sits between East and West, I thought that she was perhaps on the border between insanity and genius, as the saying goes.

"Right, so my set," she continued, returning to her previous train of thought. "It's about the life we live here. I want to leave it open for other interpretations, but generally, I'm referring to the way that young people *are* the future and that if we continue to live in a world that does not hold up to the promises made by the previous generations, then young people will be *forced* to create the very world that we were originally promised. The poem is a call to action for young people to encourage them to step up and take what they deserve. To live the good life that they were supposed to have! For us to criticize the systems under which we live so that we can rebuild what we must. Then, finally, we can enjoy life rather than being forced to fight for it. To be free of the burdens inherited by this society, to be welcomed to make our own way no matter how different we are, because we're each uniquely strong and have a lot to offer the world — I'm sorry. I'm going on and on. I said I would leave it to interpretation, and here I am imposing my perspective on you. I'll stop."

"No, it's okay," I said, laughing. "I like hearing your thoughts. It's already cleared up a lot for me."

Rather than continuing, she started fiddling with the handle of her tote bag.

"You know," I told her. "It seems that I really do connect with your poem. I admit that I didn't get it right away, but I must have understood what you were getting at. It's a more rebellious, or rather, a more driven perspective than my own, but it was still interesting to hear. I just wanted to thank you for sharing those spirited thoughts of yours."

She relaxed her shoulders, her demeanor softening. "Are you going to respond to my call to action?" she asked. I noted the hope in her voice.

"Zamanı geldi," I said and stood up. "If you'll allow *me* to be a little poetic, I think I am overdue for a renaissance of the self, so to speak. The reclaiming of my life, calling back all the little pieces of my soul that I had fragmented over the years, in hopes of finding my way forward. Maybe I'm finally in a place to take it on now. Toss out what doesn't work, salvage what deserves to stay, rebuild what I must. I think I might have already joined your fight."

She grabbed a pocket-sized notebook and pencil from her bag and started quickly jotting down a few sentences. "That's a good line ..." she mumbled to herself.

"I'll leave you to your writing, but can I know your name? If your movement takes flight, I want to be able to read about you."

"I'm Dilek, and thanks for liking my poem."

She gave me a quick handshake and returned to her notebook.

I walked away then and joined the line of people waiting to enter Ayasofya before it closed. I hoped I wasn't too late.

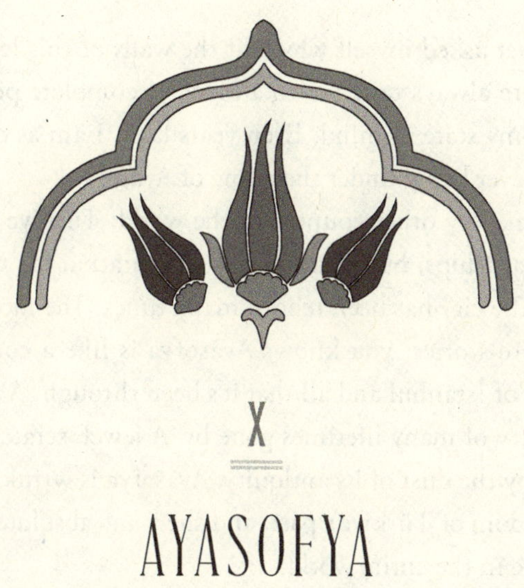

X

AYASOFYA

One special place in İstanbul had changed frequently throughout the years, but I always like to visit, no matter its state. It's a place where the world's affairs don't concern me, where important decisions don't exist, where stress isn't a part of life. It's a good place. I can go there to plan out my next steps or to ignore my burdens completely. A place that feels like it was made for me, where only I can go and breathe air meant for my lungs and cleanse myself of practicality and anxiety.

Passing the deep green marbled columns on either side of the entryway, I stepped into the sanctuary that was Ayasofya.

I've never asked myself why, but the walls of this legendary structure always take me to a place of complete peace, no matter my state of mind. Even years later, I am as comfortable as ever being under the dome of Ayasofya.

Like every other country in the world, Türkiye has suffered hardships, but İstanbul has a reputation for resurrections. The city has been reborn many times. The more scars, the more stories, you know? Ayasofya is like a condensed version of İstanbul and all that it's been through. A tangible summary of many lifetimes gone by. A jewel, scratched and veiled by the dust of its antiquity, Ayasofya is wrinkled with the wisdom of Türkiye's past, and she is my absolute favourite place in the entire world.

Ayasofya has had the title of church, then mosque, and even museum. Who knows what she is called now, she is renamed so frequently. Among all others, I feel that she understands transitions the best, because change has altered her very walls. She is a place that hushes concerns and conceals secrets. She is silent, and yet the stone stairs alone could tell you countless tales. Chapters of chaos, massacres, and invasions, but also love, harmony, and victory. Really, Ayasofya knows how to survive. When I'm here, I feel like I'm in the house of a trusted mentor. She has seen it all, but still she stands, stronger than before. Her walls and floors and hardy windows haven't been destroyed by violence. She lived. She lives. When I'm here, I feel like I could live forever, too.

I suppose that I gravitate toward her strength because so often I've been placed in the role of the strong one. But even resilient people need time to rest and other people to depend on. In many of my relationships, I have been forced to take on the role of balance, stability, consistency. When a friend is hesitating about what to do, when a relative can't handle their emotions, or when a colleague confides in me, I'm trusted to hold safe and abundant and timeless space. I hold their hands through their trials, and I share my own wisdom and help them find ways to carry on. I've been nicknamed "The Teacher," but not because I know a lot — I definitely don't always have the answer, and I admit this openly. This title has been gifted to me because I'm stable amid chaos. I'm often patient and tolerant in times of unease. I can lead while letting others walk ahead of me.

Ayasofya acts in that way for me. She is like the pillar that I can rest on when life's roads become too long and exhausting. She is one of *my* teachers, and she helped instill these skills in me.

Ayasofya's stone floor is not smooth but is instead dented by the footsteps of so many over several centuries. Evidence of millions of soldiers, worshippers, visitors — now long gone. The painted centre brings to life visions of richly clothed emperors, sultans, conquerors, each ordained in this very hall. Inside, one stands on the same floor where Constantine once stood. Ayasofya's elaborate mosaic walls are supported by arched corridors. I have leaned on the columns there, which have held Ayasofya together through earthquakes, supporting the domes from collapsing on those who dwell within. I have often wondered how she could be so durable — I wanted to learn more from her strength.

Sometimes, when faced with a tough situation, I will freeze. After the initial shock passes, usually fleeting, I assess a situation and judge what actions are appropriate. I can think clearly and critically when problem-solving, and apparently, I do it quickly, though my reactions always feel much slower in my own mind. I don't hesitate for long, and so far, I've made good calls. I hold my ground, and I can do it on behalf of others, too. I have always aimed to show my friends and family the same respect and care that I've learned to cultivate for myself. I share with them the choices that I have made in achieving a version of me that I hold in high regard. I think to myself, *If I were someone perfectly loving, cherished, deserving of all the good things that life has to offer, if I were to toss aside my insecurities and faults, what decision would I make in a given situation?*

Inside Ayasofya's walls, the journey of life doesn't really matter. When I am there, for a moment as brief as a deep inhale, I am free to just live. I have no burdens on my shoulders, but no dreams for the future. It is neither stressful nor hopeful, miserable nor exciting. I don't know what that feeling is called. I don't know what the people around me are doing and thinking or feeling, but I also don't care. The world here is silent, and I can hold it in my hands. I suppose this is what we mean by peace? Or is this what we call happiness? Euphoria? This fleeting moment, when the air smells of your favourite things, when the lights are glowing rather than glaring, and when time doesn't stop but waits for you. Life is vibrant. Alive. And I want to stay in this moment for the rest of my days. But I can't, of course. Time flees. Ayasofya breathes again and lets me go upon her exhale. But I know this feeling is what I've been searching for, what I've been chasing after. Now, on this day, it is warm and familiar, but completely elusive to me. Why in the world is Ayasofya the only place with this feeling, and how could I take it with me, outside her walls?

The low-hanging candlelit chandeliers cast warmth over the visitor below. Here, spirituality envelops you. A sanctuary for any person, at any time, for any reason. Ayasofya has housed the weak and lost, equipping people with security and purpose. She is a protector. A building that provides reassurance and rehabilitation. I wondered if she would be so generous as to lend some of that to me.

Whether I am Teacher, Guide, Friend, or Stranger, I know that it would be unlikely for me to be called the same name as Ayasofya. "Protector" seems like a title that I would never merit in this lifetime; to me, it feels almost divine. I might share similar qualities, but only fragments. The ability to look out for others, to sacrifice the self for the greater good, to be both strong shield and wise mentor. I bow to her, grateful to remain under her care. Whichever nicknames or titles I am assigned, I still feel as if my job is not yet finished and cannot be defined. Life moves fast, and I'm just trying to keep up.

"Ayasofya," I whispered to the marble steps as I made my way upstairs. "I have a confession to make, or a prayer that needs to be said. I'm not quite sure, to be honest."

She didn't answer, of course, but I continued.

"My chaotic thoughts overwhelm me. I am no pilgrim, and I am not really a religious devotee, but would you lend a listening ear to one of your own?"

A chanting rhythm began, long, single notes that extended into every corner of the space. A serene azan filled Ayasofya. It bounced off the flawless glass, the slippery marble, the rugged stone. It hummed inside my ears, reaching to their very cores. It was not loud, but it echoed. It occupied my mind and silenced my thoughts. It even quieted the crowd that had gathered in the main hall below.

I waited until the azan finished, noticing the new steadiness of my breathing.

"Ayasofya." I traced the cold stone wall with my hand as I walked the upper floor. "Maşallah, you still amaze me," I admitted. "Such a warm welcome after so many years away."

She continued to be silent.

"This visit is not like the last. I'm a little broken this time, but also stronger than I've ever been. I've grown quite a bit, actually. I think you'd be proud of me. I've been thinking about this worthless feeling, a brokenness inside — it's a relentless problem. I'm trying to fix it, but —"

Don't you think that's more interesting?

"More interesting ...?"

Why do you try to fix brokenness, as if that is the only answer?

The voice was in my head; I knew it, and yet I was surprised.

Look at me. I do not hide my scars, and you love me for it. Why do you try to erase the parts of yourself that you have not yet learned how to love?

It was my turn to be silent.

Like kintsugi, like the mosaics on my walls, you can highlight the broken pieces in shining gold. The brokenness is what makes us who we are.

"Ayasofya?" I whispered, astounded.

I am you, you know that. You already know it all.

"But I feel like I've wasted my time —"

Nothing has been wasted.

"My life must get better than this —"

Su akar, yolu bulur.

"The years spent living a boring, routine life. I've been robbed —"

You have been saved.

"I've …?" I let it sink in. "I was saved," I said, a glimmer of realization slowly growing in my mind. "I was protected?"

Everything has its time, you know that. You already know it all.

I looked out the window to the Sultan Ahmet Mosque that photographers admire so much. "Nothing has been wasted," I repeated to myself.

Everything has its time.

"I will have my time."

• • •

At the upper balcony, the halls were brighter. Each dust particle caught in the light from the window carried with it my concerns and regrets but soon disappeared into the darkness. The air was sweet here. Golden hour sunrays gently touched my skin. It felt like kindness. My thoughts remained light for the remainder of my visit.

Passing the crowds, I reached the gardens and whispered a final goodbye.

"Thank you for letting me stay where I am welcome," I said quietly.

She didn't respond.

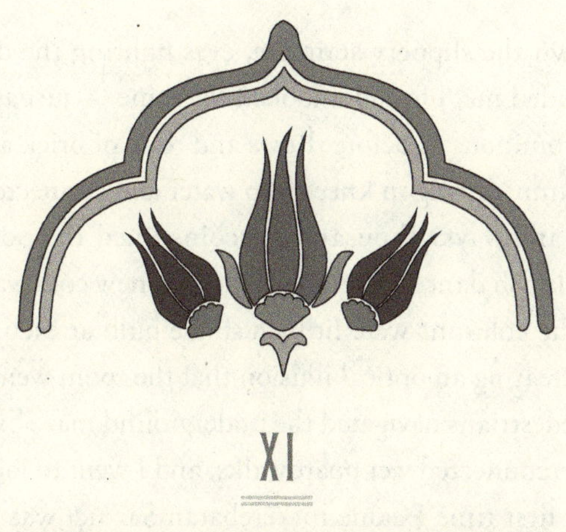

XI

YEREBATAN SARNICI

I crossed the street and bypassed the long lineup of tourists waiting to enter Yerebatan Sarnıcı. One of the perks of having a Turkish citizenship card is that you get to join the shorter Citizen Ticket Line at historic places — and you receive discounted entry fees. I wondered if I had accumulated enough sun-kissed colour throughout my day or if the attendant would give me any grief when comparing my ID card to my still-pale skin. Happily, the ticket attendant was pleased to let me in but warned me that they were closing in twenty minutes and would reopen later. A quick look around the dark and dewy cistern was all I wanted.

Down the slippery staircase, eyes fighting the dim that surrounded me, I found it looked the same — just as crowded and ominous as before. Rows and rows of brick and marble columns sitting in knee-deep water and connected at the top by archways. Thousands of coins lined the pool floor, and little fish danced around whenever a new coin was tossed over. The columns were lit by a single bulb at each of their bases, creating an optical illusion that the room went on forever. Pedestrians navigated the underground maze by following interconnected wet boardwalks, and I went to join them.

The first time I came to Yerebatan Sarnıçı was also the first time I journalled about a trip. I was nine years old and so excited to see this noted tourist spot. For some reason, I thought I'd never get the chance to return, so I wrote it all down. I recorded every little detail and how I felt about them — my commentary just kept going. Who would have thought that Nergiz and I would return to Basilica Cistern almost every year after. We loved coming here. It was always so mysterious to us. Random drops of water plopped into the reserve below. Photos turned out blurry from the dim light. You could walk endlessly above water but arrive nowhere. My favourite part was trying to reach the Medusa heads, which are these marble sculptures in the far corner of the cistern. I would stare into their eyes, tempting fate, wondering when they would quit their charade and suddenly awaken and turn me to stone. Nergiz always searched for the marble Tear Column — a singular, uniquely patterned column that looks like it's crying. We always thought it looked more like a tree, so we called it the Tree Column, like a discretely hidden tree somewhere in the dark forest of the cistern.

Reaching the centre boardwalk network, I saw new modern art installations sitting in the water. I passed stone-carved figures that cast ghostly shadows onto the walls behind them and also colourful dancing lights that shone through mythology-themed glass sculptures. I spent time admiring them all and along the way saw an artist at one of the boardwalk's edges. A much older woman was there, painting at a foldable easel. She sported white hair tied into a loose bun, partially covered by a vibrantly patterned headscarf, and wore a rose-patterned shalwar. Every part of her was adorned with thin gold jewellery, a stark contrast to her flowy and casual clothes. She looked sparkly in the dim lighting. Her paintbrush shook as she blended a new colour on her palette, but it steadied again the moment she approached the canvas. She captured the space beautifully, highlighting the reddish-yellow brick that reflected in the water below, giving dimension to this black hole of a place. Her eyes were cast low. I couldn't tell if she looked sad or was focused on her task.

"It's stunning, Hocam," I said quietly from behind her. I didn't want to spook her.

"EHH?" she said loudly and squinted at my mouth. Her eyes were a gorgeous green, encircled by wrinkles and contrasting sharply against her very tan skin.

I picked up a slight dialect change with only a single sound. I thought that I might be speaking with a Romani, but it didn't feel right to ask outright. She could just be from a different region of Türkiye. I repeated the compliment a little louder.

"Ahh, I hear you now. Thank you, akıllı çocuğum benim," she said with a grin. "I love when art admires art."

"Me? Art? Teyze, your eyes must be tired after painting for so long in this dark room," I said dismissively.

"What do you mean? Each person is a work of art."

"I'm really nothing special —"

"Can you imagine if one of Monet's paintings were able to speak and said to us, 'Oh no, no, really, I'm only a canvas! Nothing special.' Seriously? Are you challenging an old lady right now? Mothers and elders everywhere would be disappointed," she huffed.

"So … you like Monet, too?" I asked nervously.

"Don't change the subject."

"I'm sorry," I whimpered. Did she verbally slap me just now for not taking a compliment? "You must have been painting a long time — your work looks so masterful."

"Not as long as others." She examined her palette. "What are you good at?"

"I — I'm not too sure, not painting though."

"Let's try this again," the artist countered. "What do you enjoy doing?"

"That's not the same question, Teyze," I challenged, though I tried to keep a lighthearted tone.

She gave me a knowing smile. "My child. When we are excited about something, we naturally glow when we do it." She gestured to her painting, then to her own face. "Others mistake that glow to mean that we are good at it, but really, we just look happy or confident. We practise things that we like and get a little good at it over time, sure, but that's not what really sells it; it's the pleasure we get from the task. So, what do you enjoy doing?"

I thought about it. The answer wasn't coming to mind right away, and I wondered if it was connected to my whole journey to revisit İstanbul.

"You know," the artist said, "I think a stranger's mind is like a museum that I've never been to. I want to admire every artwork in their gallery, learn about it, reflect on it. I use their memories to make art collections of my own. So, tell Deren Teyze about that tiny spark of a thought you just had so that I can add it to my collection."

"I — I enjoy hearing stories," I said honestly, before the thought had even finished forming in my mind.

"Ah, a good listener. You are approachable and trustworthy." She gave a look of interest that shot straight through me. "Why did you hesitate?"

"I haven't been very happy lately, so I can't really think of what I enjoy right now."

"Hmm." She looked at me curiously. "You need to hear more stories, then?"

"Maybe. I do think they have been helping me feel better."

"I understand that sadness can blind us to good things," she said, putting down her palette and brush. "I imagine that it is like trying to admire a beautiful garden, but at nighttime, and not the kind of night with a striking full moon or millions of stars. Something like that, right? The flowers' beauty doesn't quite come across, at least not as well as it would if sunshine was filtering through the clouds. You need the right stories to light the garden."

"Yes, Teyze, I think you get it." I appreciated all her pretty metaphors.

"Hopefully, those stories can also help bring some glow to your skin," she said with a glint in her eye. "Why are you so pale? I mean, it's not that bad, but your Turkish and your appearance just don't match ..."

"Teyze," I grumbled, irritated. I barely refrained from rolling my eyes.

"May I?" She reached for my hands.

I gave her my hands, palms up, wondering if she was about to give a reading, or maybe she was going to inspect my skin's chemistry.

"Oh no," she said, flipping my hands over and just holding them. "I don't do palm readings. Fal, yes, but we don't have that right now. So just a brief chat between neighbours."

I nodded. She gently brushed her thumb across my knuckles. Her eyes were at once captivating and cast in shadow. Her wrinkles deepened suddenly, like a sky turning overcast.

"I'm sorry," she began. "How painful. To feel lonely and hopeless is a struggle indeed. But you are not the first and not the last to endure such a thing."

I swallowed.

"And, you are not lost," she added.

"Sorry?" I asked, a little taken aback. Did I give it away somehow, or did she just know?

"You think you are lost, correct? Moving without direction, aimless, in want of a goal to fulfill your purpose?"

"I suppose."

"You are unsure of what to change, what to try, what to do. You feel lost, am I wrong?"

"You are correct, Teyze. I am bored, unhappy, confused even."

"Take it day by day," she offered. "I understand you also seek guidance from others — a humble and good decision. Asking others for their input is a strength as long as you know how to filter what information is useful and what isn't."

"Thank you, I am trying to learn from my community," I admitted.

"Good for you, but don't forget that you are also a community."

"What do you mean?"

"We are each the sum total of our experiences," she began. "The traits that make up your identity — you are the combination of several people over many generations. Take the best from them and learn the lessons from the rest of it. You carry teachings and triumphs and skills that go back hundreds of years. Spend time with yourself. The more you engage, the more they can teach you, the more you build yourself up, the more you become who you are meant to be. You yourself are the accumulation of a living and growing community. You are made of legends."

I nodded.

"You are not lost, Yolcu. You are not standing still, either." She smiled again. "You are moving, each and every day. The skies will not stay in darkness forever. You will be able to see your way again," she said reassuringly, still holding my hands.

"Where am I supposed to go?" I asked. "My life is not going anywhere, so how am I supposed to change that? I feel too warm here, but cold there, and not satisfied anywhere. Not to mention, I can't see what is directly in front of my eyes. Everyone talks as if the correct direction is obvious. Every time I think I've found my way, it doesn't lead me very far. It doesn't feel right or true or complete. This happens to me again and again. Why hasn't it ever worked out for me? I see the best out of everyone that I know, and yet I still can't get this part right? I'm awake while they're all asleep, but I'm the one who is uncertain? At this point, I doubt I can even recognize what is meant for me or trust myself to choose it."

Deren Teyze listened intently, watching me panic in front of her.

"I'm sorry," I said, embarrassed. "People sometimes have trouble following my thoughts. I'm a little puzzled about it all, or maybe just desperate."

"I do not have trouble following your mind. Even if I was blind, I'd know how to get to you. I have already been to where you are now and have moved on. You see the lines around my eyes? You will get them, too! You have a lifetime ahead," she said warmly. "But you're going to wish you had my sense of style, that's for sure."

We laughed, but I was still ruminating over what to do next.

"Let me put it like this," Deren Teyze began, as if still reading my thoughts. "Let's use the analogy that we are walking in a forest. We are on a path that leads us through ups and downs, as is the nature of life. The pursuit of happiness. You know it, right?"

I hummed in agreement.

"We pass others on their own path," she continued. "All of us in the same forest, moving in the same general direction.

Some are ahead of us, some behind. Some are thriving, while others are learning lessons that the rest of us have already learned. We come to crossroads, which are the big decisions in life, and must choose what we want to do next. Everyone gains experience at their own pace, walking their own path. We are told not to compare ourselves to others, as we are each on our own unique journey.

"And then at the end of our path, we reach the big shiny outcome, the fulfillment as we approach death. Everyone is always trying to reassure others to stay on the path. They say, 'Keep moving forward!' and other expressions like that, right?"

I nodded.

"This is incorrect," she said calmly.

I raised an eyebrow, curious to know where this was going.

"I mean, it is partially correct, but it's an incomplete analogy," she continued. "It is true that we cannot go backwards. We cannot travel to the past, we can only look back at it. The road behind cannot be travelled by us again; however, the analogy gives the impression that there is only one correct and straight path to our goal. I believe this to be false. It is what leads to people, just like you, thinking they took a wrong turn, scared to make the next decision in their lives. If you are unsure of your purpose or are hesitating about where to go, then you supposedly fell off this narrow path and became 'lost.' It is a fearful thought and not completely accurate."

"What is true then, Teyze?"

"What if I told you that the whole point is not to take one straightforward path in life?" She spoke carefully, as if she were revealing a secret. "Instead, try as many different roads as you can. Travel to the east, to the west, straight ahead. Take on the twists and turns with enthusiasm. The goal is to experience all the best things that life can offer. If something is not working, go seek a different direction. Explore. People should aim to 'get lost' on purpose!"

It was a hopeful thought — the idea that being unsure what to do next was actually the right place to be all along. Still, it was a new perspective that I was not used to considering. Or the idea that we are each a walking community — I liked the sound of that one, too. It felt a lot less gloomy, the thought that you are not completely alone even when you're by yourself. I was thinking that maybe this auntie was a compilation of several generations of healers, travellers, old friends from past lifetimes. It was my turn to smile.

"I like this version of the story, Deren Teyze."

"Oh, you must be happier now then? The story-lover heard another one, and I collected another piece of art." She let go of my hands.

I took her right hand in mine and raised it first to my chin, then my forehead.

"It was a pleasure, Teyze. Thank you," I said with sincerity.

"Likewise," she said. "Go on now, yolcu yolunda gerek!" At that, Deren Teyze returned to her easel, and I to the world outside the cistern.

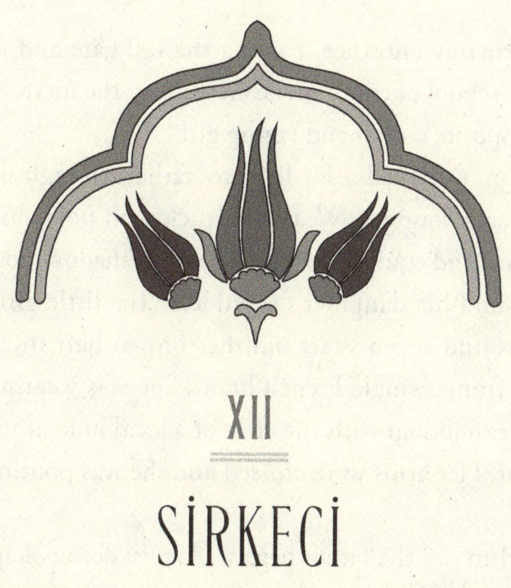

XII

SİRKECİ

I wandered toward Sirkeci's historic train station, where the Orient Express connected İstanbul and the rest of the world. Passing its stained-glass windows, I noted the sky — it would be dark soon. I didn't have much time left before I had to be at my aunt's place for the family dinner. I'd have to gather up my remaining energy to chat with the wedding party or fake feeling jetlagged and leave early. Either way, tomorrow's festivities were going to be a real challenge if I didn't get some rest early tonight. One last stop probably wouldn't make too big of a difference, so I circled below to the Marmaray entrance, passing the toll gate and merging with the school of commuters. Getting on the metro, I found a seat opposite a man and young girl.

The man looked a lot like my father, though probably thirty years younger. Wearing a tucked-in polo shirt, dark blue jeans, and equipped with five o'clock shadow, he had one arm around his daughter's shoulders. The little girl looked to be around seven years old, her brown hair unravelling slightly from a single French braid. She was wearing a perfectly clean judogi with the crest of a local judo academy on the front. Her arms were crossed and she was pouting at the floor.

"Tatlım ..." the father began. "Are we doing okay?"

She shook her head grumpily.

"Has it been tough lately? Feeling like too much?"

She looked up at him, tears gathering in her eyes.

"It's supposed to be difficult, you know," he continued, gently rubbing her shoulder. "Things that are worth it are never easy."

"But I'm trying so hard!" she said in that tiny shout that kids do.

"I know, and you're doing so good."

"No, I'm not. I'm not good enough," she insisted.

"Why do you say that?"

"It's so easy for my friends, but it's hard for me."

"It only looks that way —"

"Defne is so fast!" the girl interrupted. "She always gets the new move right the first time. I have to try so many times before I get it right."

"I bet Defne admires your discipline," the father countered. "And how often you practise to get better."

"I don't know …"

"Everyone is working to improve something, Elacım. You can't always see it from the outside."

"They're too good. It's not fair. I'm trying so hard." She sounded defeated.

She accidentally made eye contact with me. I smiled at her, but Ela looked down and started twisting the fabric belt in her hands.

"I will teach you about self-compassion," her father said. He gave her a side hug. "It means finding nice things to say to yourself instead of saying mean things. We'll practise together."

"I'm not mean …" Ela said quietly, cheeks turning even more pink.

"You said you are not good enough," he reminded her. "That is being mean to yourself. It makes me so sad to hear, because I think you're perfect."

She kept pouting but started swinging her legs at the compliment.

The man reminded me of my own parents. They always tried to be encouraging when I was feeling down. Not a lot of people understood me, and my parents didn't always get it right, either. Still, they were pretty good at sensing when I needed support. Like when I was in school, around Ela's age. I didn't get very good grades back then. In fact, my grades were consistently dropping. When my parents asked what was wrong, I told them I felt stupid because the other kids in my class told me that I was. I believed them, because I had no reason not to. I realized later that those kids just didn't understand me, and my teachers were no help. Looking back, I would say they were most likely threatened or maybe even confused by me, because I had been brought up differently. My Turkish culture taught me to have a community-centric mindset, aiming to help and support others. In the Western world, there is more competition — a greater focus on the individual and on each person getting ahead. My culture taught me to be respectful to everyone, especially authority figures and elders, so I prioritized being obedient. For my classmates, being mischievous in school was a rite of passage. Teachers always suspected their students had ulterior motives. I was never that person. I was "other" from the rest of the kids my age, and they made sure I knew it. Renard, the boy from Galata Tower, had reminded me of the sort of person that had surrounded me when I was growing up.

My parents were angered to hear that I had been made to feel less than welcome at school. I received a hearty speech about how my intelligence was greater than that of all of the other kids combined. They convinced me enough that I returned to school, determined to try again. Little did my parents know, they had managed to ignite something inside me. The students and teachers didn't get much kinder or more understanding as the years went on, but I gained points in resilience and perseverance. I became an honour roll student, something I maintained all the way through university. I graduated at the top of my class.

"Ela, when something is challenging, it's very easy to be hard on yourself," the father began. "But I want you to remember that you are very capable. My daughter is so smart, kind, beautiful, and much more. She can do anything, but that does not mean that it will be easy. Some things take time and need practise, and some things simply will never work out. You need to learn to try your best, no matter what happens in the end. If you say nicer things to yourself, then the hard things might feel a little easier to do. Does that make sense, tatlım?"

Ela nodded.

"Try saying something nice about yourself," the father pushed.

The daughter searched the metro advertisements above my head for inspiration, her legs still swinging. She soon proclaimed, "I have a very good father."

"*Aghhh*," the father beamed and gripped the collar of his polo shirt. "My daughter! How could you use my own skills against me?"

"It's true!" she said, trying to muffle her laugh with her hands. "None of the other students have their Baba come to practice. You always come. I'm glad you're here."

Another phrase that I loved to hear: "I'm glad you're here." Those who suffer with their mental fortitude know that being told how you are appreciated and valued, even for the littlest of things, makes a huge difference. During some of the hardest moments of my life, I have felt isolated and hopeless. There were a couple years where I couldn't find work and struggled to pay my own way. I couldn't buy groceries or put gas in my car, let alone buy a house or travel. Like most people, I have also experienced heartbreak a few times, not finding the loving and aligned partnership that every person deserves. I had become separated from certain close friends, too, people that I once considered family. We had outgrown each other, but that didn't make it hurt any less. Of course, I have lost relatives, from illness and age and trauma. Each of their deaths left behind a deep wound, and I replay our memories often in an effort to keep feeling their company. Life is not easy, and I don't care if people say otherwise. I do not compare people's pain; instead, I simply accept when they tell me about it. When my soul was suffering, the negative thoughts pretty much consumed me. I needed someone outside myself to get involved. I needed someone to tell me that I mattered.

Not too long ago, I received a lot of bad news within a very short period of time. Beyond the impact on my mental health, I noticed more fatigue than usual as my body got thrown into the mix. I was burnt out from trying to survive during a difficult year. My personal life took a critical hit, my professional life was made to take a knee, my physical health was neck-deep in its own trials, and my spiritual self was struggling to keep me all in one piece. I couldn't fix any part of it immediately and instead had to wait for time to pass. I hated not being able to change any part of my circumstances at that time. I couldn't find a job. I wasn't able to pay my bills. I didn't have weekend getaways to sweep me away from reality. I was tired all the time. I was afraid.

Often I would wake up crying and try to fall asleep again with my heart racing. Randomly throughout the day, I would get lightheaded and nauseated, thinking this was it for me. This was all I would ever be. Every day this new routine repeated, not getting any easier — I was trapped in a prison of self-hatred and fear, which only fed and strengthened the cycle. I have always tried to push through tough times alone, and I have become pretty good at it over the years, but there are limits to hyper-independence. This was one of those cases.

Thankfully, my inner circle stepped in to share the burden. The people closest to me, who stayed by my side, who knew about this low point in my life, showered me with positive messages, distractions, and hopeful ideas to look forward to later on. Expressions like "I'm glad you're here" were ammunition against the negative thoughts that worked hard to infiltrate and overtake my mind. These days, I never hesitate to tell someone how glad I am to know them, because you never know when someone needs to hear it. Those sweet words saved my life more than once.

"Tatlı kızım!" the father said, smiling and hugging her tighter.

"Baba?" Ela said hesitantly.

"Hmm?"

"Why do you come to judo practice?" she asked. "You're the only one who comes and stays for the whole practice."

"To watch you be amazing, of course," he said casually. "And to be there in case you need me."

"Need you for what?" she asked. "You can't join the class, you're not a student."

"Like, when your belt gets untied because you keep fiddling with it," he said with a wink and a nudge.

"I know how to tie my belt!" she exclaimed, and then tied it immediately before our eyes.

"Excellent, well done!" He laughed and gave her a pat on the head. "I can also help you when you are being mean to yourself, right?"

Ela nodded, looking pensive once again.

"If you ever feel down, let me take care of it, okay, tatlım? Just come talk to me."

Those last words there, they are what shine a light in those pitch-black tunnels of the mind. Hearing "Let me take care of it" from someone who genuinely cares for you is like nothing else. When your burdens start to multiply, when they get too heavy for one person to carry — boulders balancing on your shoulders, threatening to topple you — it's a relief for someone to willingly come along and remove some of that weight. A whole landslide can be avoided. Without having to ask, without having to interrogate someone's intentions — that modest bit of assistance has a mighty impact. It shows support that remains unmatched, in my eyes.

One morning before heading to work, it was freezing cold and my car wouldn't start. I was having a rough week and knew nothing about cars, making this minor obstacle a big inconvenience. I had a splitting headache, too. My neighbour was leaving for a morning jog at the same time — in the dead of winter, no less, those wild Canadians — and asked me what was wrong. I explained the situation and he said, "Let me take care of it," before disappearing into his garage. He tried to give my car battery a jump, but it wasn't working. He then told me to get into his truck so that he could take me to work on time. He also asked for my keys so that he could keep trying to troubleshoot the car — he said he would call his mechanic friend to give him a hand. I gave in. I released all my care to him. I didn't wish to question whether he was really going to help me or not; I just blindly trusted that he would resolve things for me. I didn't have the capacity to handle it myself. Carrying more stress than simple car troubles in the back of my mind, I could barely keep from crying in his car. He called me later that day to tell me that the car was working again. He offered me a ride home from work, but I declined. I took the bus home and found a well-working car in my driveway when I arrived.

When the sun goes down in my soul, the shadows creep in and have room to roam. I don't know about you, but I find that during such times, my self-reflection becomes too honest, almost beastly. Unforgiving. Pain thrives in that kind of environment. With my car, I probably could have figured it out by myself, but why do it alone when help is available? Why walk in the darkness when a light is within reach?

"Aslanım, Elacım," the father said. "Look, it's our stop."

Ela stopped swinging her feet and jumped down from her seat. I got up, too, and we exited the metro together. When I arrived at street level, the ground was wet, and it didn't feel so warm anymore. It must have rained briefly. My phone pinged — I looked to see that I'd missed a call from my sister when I was underground. I dialled back the bride-to-be before continuing my route.

"Hey!" she answered right away. "Just wanted to check and make sure you're still good for our meet-up time for dinner? The last I heard you were at baggage claim. What have you been up to for the whole day?"

"Just wandering around the city."

"All day? It's so hot. Please don't get heat stroke, I need you for all of *this*." I imagined her waving a hand around in the air. "So, stay out of the sun! Oh wait, I guess it's a little late to say that now."

"Have you relaxed at all, or has it been only craziness and last-minute preparations?" I asked. "You had wanted the day to yourself, no?"

"Well, I told the skies that I wanted to cry today, and they started without me, but I have some 'me' time now. Otherwise, nothing to report. Everything is pretty much ready to go."

"Why were you crying, Nergiz?"

"Oh, you know, new beginnings and all. It's emotional."

"I see."

"Really, it's scary. Uncharted waters are scary for me. But also exciting, don't get me wrong. I'm equally scared and excited."

"I'm proud of you."

"Why? That's sudden. I mean, I know you love me, but that's nice of you to say."

"Uncharted waters," I echoed. "It scares you, but you're trying your best anyway."

"Well yeah, I mean, should I just survive life or should I try living it?"

"Hmm." I let her words soak in.

"Let's give this life a go, shall we?" she said enthusiastically. "Try our best, right?"

"I suppose you're right."

"See you later!" she chimed.

"See you later," I said and hung up the phone.

• • •

My sister was a gem. Nergiz had a way of making even the muddiest of things clear. She had always been the more direct one, while I was the one who thinks too much. A balance of the two of us would have probably been ideal.

The sun was gone now, but it wasn't dark yet. I looked up and saw the stars starting to appear in the twilight. Over the next half hour, İstanbul at night would descend from the skies, and the city would be adorned in a different kind of glow.

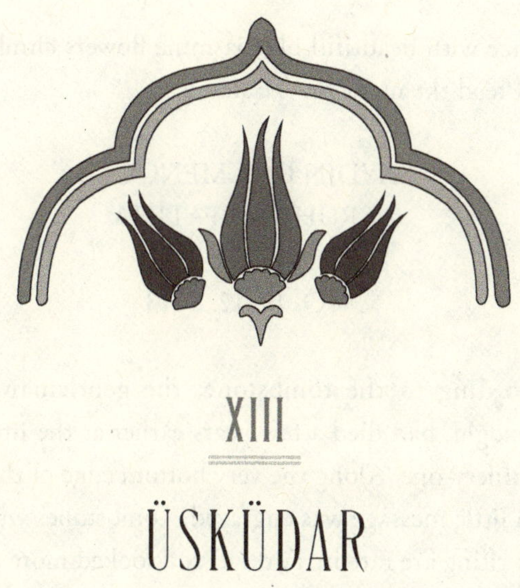

XIII

ÜSKÜDAR

Before it got totally dark out, I decided to take a detour through one of the cemeteries. I was in another busy district, and I knew that the cemetery would be less crowded and noisy than the street. Turkish cemeteries feature white marble graves, partially aligned next to each other, interlaced with lovely overgrown native flowers. Organized chaos. They are like walking through paradise, if paradise was overrun with plants and had smudged tombstone writings. Following the barely visible dirt path through the greenery and marble, one tombstone in particular caught my eye. It didn't look too different from the others, except that it was at the base of an iron fence with beautiful blue jasmine flowers climbing the metal. I read the name on the stone.

AYDIN GÖÇMENOĞLU
RUHUNA FATİHA
D. 25. 05. 1922
Ö. 19. 12. 2013

According to the tombstone, the gentleman, Aydın Göçmenoğlu, had died a few years earlier at the impressive age of ninety-one. Along the very bottom edge of the tombstone, a little message was engraved. Tombstones with additional writing are rare in Türkiye, so I looked more closely.

Gençler buyursun. İtiraflar, XIII.

It was definitely not a Quran verse, but I wasn't too sure what it was referring to. I pulled out my phone and performed a quick internet search, which took me to a long list of texts with the same title, written by various authors over several centuries. I spotted a link to an eBook of short stories by a writer whose name matched the tombstone. It was published the year before his death. I turned to chapter thirteen and read the section that stood out with a pretty border around it.

It is okay to be sad, but not for long; there are still places you must go.

That weight on your shoulders looks a little heavy. Why don't you give it to me? Without it, you will travel further. I have no use for something that heavy, so it really is okay to give it to me. The living have a hard time healing from their pain, but the dead can easily free themselves of it. So, give it all to me. I will toss it into the nothingness for you.

There, now we are both free of it. Before you continue on your way again, my young friend, just remember something for me — there are more reasons to live than there are to die.

You didn't expect me to say it so bluntly, right? I know it can feel like a lot, all piling up on you. Do not try to keep hold of it all. Trust me, it becomes too heavy. Some pieces will fall and that will hurt others, too. Guilty. I confess that I speak from experience. Believe me, only hold on to the most important pieces because they will feel like nothing to carry. Let the rest go.

Now go live weightlessly. A last bit of wisdom from this stubborn old man, who learned that lesson too late in life.

• • •

I remembered the kind brown eyes of the rug weaver and the hundreds of rugs that adorned her shop. If you were to pile them all up, they would be quite heavy. I couldn't even imagine the weight of all that she had made and sold, what she had given away. It was a lot of rugs to make and way too much to carry around at once. Knowing the weight of a single strand of thread, it is odd to think that an individual rug could be so heavy. One rug can be too much for most people to lift alone. Then I started to think that some of us are given more threads than others. Naturally, those rugs are larger and heavier. It can't be helped — they might be impossible to carry with just your own two hands. If we were to listen to Mr. Göçmenoğlu's advice, we should set the rug down. But the weight of mine on my shoulders is at once too hard to hold and too heavy to put down without help. Now what? I stand here shaking, crumbling, unsure of what to do, desperate for a rescue. My rug is much heavier than I am prepared to carry.

A person not too far behind me cleared their throat. I turned to see a middle-aged man in dirty clothing looking at me, keeping a safe distance.

"Tanıdığınız mı?" he asked softly as he approached.

"No," I said, surprised. "Should — should I leave?" I stammered, thinking again about how I was hanging out in a cemetery.

"Maybe, I mean, why are you at the cemetery then?" the man asked.

"It caught my attention — the flowers," I said nervously. "They're my favourites." I felt my face heat up at my words. He kept his eyes focused on me. "I was passing through," I elaborated. "Usually, the gardens around here are nice to look at and much calmer than the main road."

He gave me a quick head tilt down, but kept his eyes on me. "I do my best for the families," he stated.

It clicked. His dirty clothes, his sudden appearance — he was the groundskeeper. He must have thought that I was up to no good, not having any real business visiting the dead here.

"Terribly sorry," I added quickly, and reached into my pocket for some change. "You do a tremendous job. Everything looks lovely. I'll get out of your way," I said hurriedly and handed him a tip.

The man politely refused the money with two taps to his chest. "Hoca Göçmenoğlu gets many visitors," he said. "I understand that he was a famous scholar. A young woman claiming to be a poet comes here a lot. Yesterday she came to water the flowers. Of course, I had already watered them. She talks a lot. I don't really understand her. These flowers are some of the nicer ones. They like hydrated soil, perfect for this area."

"This place is in good hands." I was impressed by his knowledge.

"I don't know what Hocam wrote in his life, but people seem to visit him often," said the groundskeeper. "It's okay if you stay a little longer, but don't water anything, it already rained."

Before I could respond, the groundskeeper's gaze shifted to something behind me. I turned to see a man sitting by a grave, blankly looking at the white stone in front of him. He was unfazed by the bumblebee doing laps around the sunglasses that sat perched atop his head.

"Actually," the groundskeeper started, "if you have no other business, perhaps you could help the man over there?"

"What can I do for him?"

"What can any of us do for him?" There was sadness in his voice. "Sit with him. Talk about the jasmine flowers. He recently lost his best friend of several decades."

"Of course," I promised the stranger, and I turned to meet another one.

The tombstone didn't look any different from the rest. It was a marble rectangle sitting in soft dirt. No name engraved on the stone yet. The soil was too new to grow anything, so a small bouquet of wildflowers decorated the stone instead. The man sitting across from it was solemn but acknowledged me right away. I sat next to him, and the bee moved on, circling the wildflowers. I noticed the man's right palm resting on his shirt pocket.

"Abi, my condolences." I placed a light hand on his shoulder.

He nodded.

"The groundskeeper told me that you knew this person a long time?"

He nodded again.

"That is a big loss. I am sorry to hear it," I said honestly.

"He won't be able to see." The man spoke hoarsely and stared at the soil. "My soul will forever be crying."

"I'm sure he knew how much you cared for him," I responded, trying to sound lighthearted for his sake. The man was clearly more upset than he let on.

"No, you don't understand. We argued. I hadn't spoken to my friend for a year."

"Argued about what?"

"I don't really remember anymore," he said, defeated. "Nothing important, looking back. We didn't talk to each other out of pure bitterness, a personality trait we both share, unfortunately." He rubbed the shirt pocket, briefly revealing a folded-up paper inside. "He must have really hated me," he added spitefully.

"What's that in your shirt pocket?" I was too curious to let it slide.

"A letter." He sighed. "He sent it to me when we finished our doctorate degrees. It's from over twenty-five years ago."

I stared at it, thinking I might see the words through the thin paper.

"It was our first time living apart," the man continued. "We had been roommates since the very first day of university. After nearly ten years in the same house, I moved away for a job. We finally separated and he sent me this letter."

"Why do you carry it with you?"

"I planned to read it when I came here." He sounded crushed already. "I haven't gotten the courage to open it yet. I have only read it once and that was when I first received it. I remember being comforted when I read it then."

"Ha gayret," I said encouragingly. "Let's do it together. Remember him today in the way that you knew him best, not in the way that you knew him last. I'd like to meet that version of him. What do you say?"

The man sighed again and stared at the marble grave ahead of him, lost in deep thought. After a moment of internal debate, he slowly removed the paper from his pocket.

"My hands were much younger the last time I opened this letter," he acknowledged, speaking more to himself. He began reading the letter aloud.

13th of January, 1988
Canım arkadaşım Özgürcim,

The house is too quiet, too clean, and too plain. I hate it. Can you imagine that I miss your sneeze that used to threaten the collapse of our walls? How I miss the way you used to spray way too much cologne in the bathroom, and we thought the bath towels would never be clean again? Who would predict that I actually want to wash your pile of dirty dishes rather than win at backgammon and have you wash them instead? How about the fact that I still do not eat breakfast unless you are the one to make it? Where are you, when you clearly belong over here? Oh yes, you have gone somewhere much better. I suppose I cannot be angry at that.

But I will be angry, just for a little while. At least give me that much, after all these years. If I can be honest, as we are such good friends, I will tell you that I sometimes find myself avoiding pieces of you since you left. I try not to stay in the kitchen, because that's where I would usually find you. I do not go to your favourite library café near Harem's pier. I do not wear red because of that one double date in Sarıyer, when you told me that I looked too good in red, noticing that your date kept staring at me instead of you. You were so frustrated. You probably do not remember it, or the way that we used to talk until late into the night, sitting on the roof and under the stars. I do not admire the skies anymore. I cannot bring myself to do a lot of things without you here. I'm really angry about that. You've ruined a lot of my favourite things.

Do not worry. There will come a time when I will not be upset with you for moving away, and I will resume doing all those things. Not today, but one day. Until then, I will imagine that you are well. I hope the internship is going okay for you and that you have time to rest. You deserve all the promotions, all the best opportunities, all the things you desire. I wish you nothing but nice things. Tell me all about what you are up to when you get the chance. Even if you run out of paper, our telepathy should still be working strong, and I will listen for it. I want to hear all about your adventures, so make your story a good one. Do your best, Özgür.

I suppose there is nothing much for me to do, except to try and do well, too. I will impress you with how much I've grown since you left. I only really care about your opinion, but don't tell my mother that. I'll write myself a good story and share it with you when I visit in the summer. You better write me back and give me at least a small update, or else I'll come and find you even sooner than June.

Stay healthy, keep going, and good luck, kardeşim.

En kısa zamanda görüşmek üzere,
Efe

P.S. You know Semiha, the little girl who lives next door and thinks you are the best person ever? (Why does she like you more, we will never know.) She came by to give you a craft that she made at school. I guess you didn't mention you were moving away, and I am not the best at comforting someone in tears — I told her you were visiting family but that I will be sure to give her present to you when you return. I'll write her a thank-you note with your name signed and slip it under their door. You owe me one now.

Next to me, Özgür struggled to take full breaths. The man's tears overwhelmed him. Eyebrows knitted and face turning red, Özgür hurriedly folded up the paper and placed it back in his shirt pocket. He didn't look at me.

"It is okay to be sad," I said quietly, remembering Mr. Göçmenoğlu's words. "You had a wonderful friendship, and Efe Abi seemed like a brother who had a lot of affection for you."

Özgür nodded.

"I'm glad you brought this letter," I said, trying to soothe him. "I feel like I got to meet an incredible man, thanks to you. I am sure that he knows how dearly you miss him. May he rest in peace."

Özgür wiped his face with his arm, taking a few deep breaths before speaking again.

"You know," he cleared his throat. "Efe ended up dating Semiha's school teacher — they got married about four years later."

I raised an eyebrow at him.

"Semiha kept crying at school when she learned that I had moved away. It lasted weeks," he explained. "Her poor mother couldn't soothe her. Efe felt so terrible that he took Semiha to school one day and went to explain to her teacher that it was all his fault. He said that he didn't do a good job telling Semiha about my moving away. In his next letter, Efe told me that the whole conversation was a blur — he only remembered that the teacher had spoken to him softly and reassuringly and that he really needed to see her again."

"What a story!" I told him, impressed at the turn of events. "He got really lucky."

"I know, I know." Özgür was smiling now, but tears still streamed down his face. We were quiet for a moment, thinking about the fateful event that led to Efe meeting his future wife.

The breeze picked up, and the tall grass swayed a little. Özgür peeked at me. He looked ready to make a confession.

"Efe's daughter told me at the funeral that he talked about me a lot," Özgür said in almost a whisper. "She said Efe had only nice things to say, but I didn't believe her. I felt too ashamed. What kind of a friend doesn't speak to you for months, doesn't even call on your birthday? Even though he didn't talk to me either, conversations go both ways. My anger left me quickly, but still, I didn't call him. He didn't deserve that."

"You owe him," I said.

"Yes, but he also —"

"In the letter, I mean, all those years ago. Efe Abi said you owed him a favour for telling Semiha that little lie to protect you. Let's assume you never paid him back. You owe him now. Repay your debt to him by putting this silly argument behind you. Forgive both him and yourself."

"That doesn't sound good enough," Özgür said skeptically. "Efe deserves more."

"Then believe his daughter," I insisted. "It sounds like Efe Abi also had no interest in arguing anymore. Let him be the older brother you remember him to be."

Özgür stared at the bouquet of flowers on Efe's grave. Eventually, he wiped his face of tears again and nodded.

"I will check in on his daughter tomorrow," Özgür said resolutely. "I'll see if she needs anything. Anything at all, I will help her."

"I like that idea."

"Thank you." Özgür patted my back.

"Abi, if you are okay with it, I'll be on my way now," I said, getting up.

Özgür gave me a small smile. "My friend, you may go. I don't need you at my side anymore, and that is the biggest compliment that I am capable of giving."

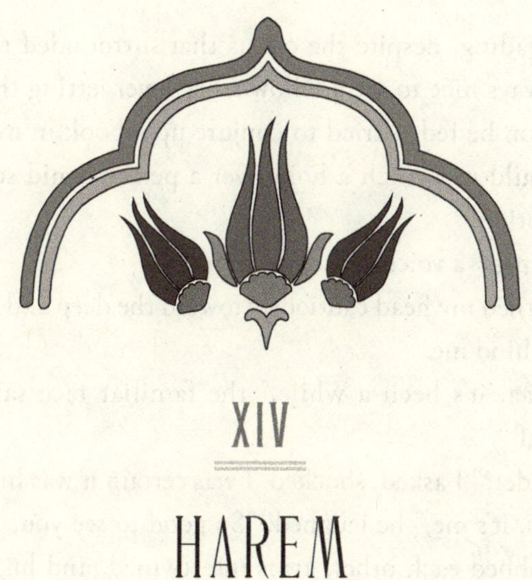

XIV

HAREM

The pier was full of energy. Foreigners and locals alike crowded benches that overlooked the crashing water. People were shouting over booming music, asking for tea refills, laughing over card games by candlelight, posing for photos with İstanbul at night reflected atop the Bosphorus. The ground was littered with sunflower seed shells, and the air smelled of apple-flavoured hookah smoke. My attention was directed toward the only calm person in the vicinity. They were seated under a streetlamp, reading a book by the edge of Harem's waterfront. They appeared immersed in their reading, despite the circus that surrounded them. It was always nice to see a fellow story-lover letting their imagination be fed. I tried to conjure up a book in my mind that could take such a hold over a person amid so much commotion.

"Deniz?" a voice called out to me.

I turned my head cautiously toward the deep and curious tone behind me.

"Aaaa, it's been a while," the familiar face said with disbelief.

"Kader?" I asked, shocked. I was certain it was him.

"Yes, it's me," he laughed. "So good to see you, Deniz!" We grabbed each other, arms intertwined, and hugged. It was maybe a decade ago that I last saw my childhood friend.

"I'm so glad to bump into you!" I said, still in awe. Out of all the places in İstanbul he could have been, among all the people, we found each other here again. He looked almost the same, except for a few threads of white through his hair and some brand-new laugh lines.

"How have you been, Kader?" I asked eagerly. "Please tell me you are well."

"What were you doing so close to the edge? You'll get wet from the waves," he said, a little concerned. He held me gently at the back of my neck. "No offense, but you look like your mind is more turbulent than the water. Why are your brows so bunched up? You have to stop that, they will stay like that, you know." He used his finger to push up the skin between my eyebrows.

"I've had quite the day," I confessed with a sigh. Suddenly, I became aware of the soreness of my feet and the aching of my back. "I've wandered all around the city and heard so many stories today. There's a lot for me to think about," I told him.

"Oh, I've been there," he said with a nod. "İstanbul has so much to say, doesn't it?"

"Mhmm. Hey, can I ask you something really quickly?"

He nodded.

"Do I look pale to you?"

"Pale?" he said, confused. "No, your skin looks fine. Why? You are not feeling well?"

"Never mind," I said, deciding to let it go. "It's dark outside, you probably can't really tell."

"Well then," Kader continued. "What are you doing back in the city, anyway? Just visiting? Are you here with family?"

"Actually, I don't know. Well, that's not true. My sister is getting married in the city, but I don't know if I will be staying after the wedding."

"Congratulations to her — I hope it is everything she wants and more."

"Thank you, Kader."

"Back to you, my indecisive friend," he teased. "I think that you are wise to hesitate at a deceivingly simple question. Care to talk to me about it? Why not stay in İstanbul for a while?"

"Ah, well, it's been so long." I tried to explain what I felt, but I didn't know how to convey my own thoughts aloud, despite having spent all day telling people about them. "I'm not sure I belong here anymore. I'm not too sure where I belong, to be honest." That last part was more to myself.

Kader gave a wide smile, revealing dimples on both sides of his face. "Is it finally your turn, Deniz? Time to figure out your next steps in life? It's the big question that we all have to ask ourselves at the end of every chapter. I guess it has come back around to plague your mind now. Which direction are you leaning toward?"

"Are we going to jump right into the big questions?" I joked, matching his good humour. "You're not even going to tell me what you've been up to for the last decade?"

"There is no such formality among old friends." He waved off my questions. "I think we need to take care of your struggle first. We'll get to my updates in a minute. Tell me what is wrong."

I looked at him and saw someone who had brought me comfort several times in my life. When I lost each of my grandparents, Kader attended every funeral and stayed by my side the whole time. He knew when to leave me alone, when to distract me, and when he had to divert other people from me. When I landed my first job and had to stay in Toronto rather than travel back to İstanbul one summer, he sent me the sweetest letter full of encouragement and reassurance that I was making the best choice for myself. I had felt regret for staying away from my relatives for so long, but his message consoled me. Then there was the time we were around ten years old, when he told me how he dreamed of living in Australia. I bawled at his declaration. I was devastated thinking about one of my closest friends moving to the other side of the world. To soothe me, he got out a notebook and sketched out an entire calendar year. He marked every special occasion where he would call me; he scheduled which days he would send me a letter and which weeks he would come back to İstanbul so that they would match up with my summer vacation from school. As we grew older, we lost touch a little, mostly because we lived so far away from one another and kept busy, but we still relayed our hellos through proxies. My care for him never wavered though, because Kader was always genuine, selfless, and self-assured. He was everything that I wanted to be.

For the first time today, I would declare my fears to a friend rather than a stranger.

"I've been feeling a little stuck in life. Or maybe … behind?" I confessed shyly.

"Ohh, gözünü seveyim," he said, irritated. "Come on, don't do that." He pulled me to a bench that was safe from the swelling waves.

"What have I done now?" I replied, keeping our light-hearted tone. "Scolding me again, are you? It is as if no time has passed from when you last lectured me."

"You are too hard on yourself. What makes you think that you are the only one going through a difficult time? Life is not that easy, and we learn that lesson almost right away. I'll tell you, too, since you brought it up, that belonging is something that a lot of people struggle with, but it is not tied to a place, just like loneliness is not relevant to your relationship status."

"I don't know," I admitted.

I thought about how Kader really did end up living in Australia, back when he was earning his philosophy degree. He followed that with an internship in Alexandria, where he learned about polytheism and wrote so many interesting articles on the subject. Every now and then, I'd search up his name and read his latest publication. Those writings had landed Kader teaching positions all over the world. He had recently come back to İstanbul and was now teaching at Boğaziçi University on a well-deserved tenure track.

"It's been years since I've been back here, but my life hasn't progressed much," I continued. "*You* look fine, *great* even. I also heard that you got a new teaching job, and I bet you'll soon be able to buy one of those fancy houses on the Bosphorus —"

"Stop. Just stop." There was bite to his words.

"What?"

"You were not there."

How had I made him angry? It would have been better if he'd just spat on me.

"You do not know what kind of life I've had," he shared. "Let me give you the short answer: You cannot summarize my experiences with just the highlights. The shadows existed, too. I had a *hard* time, Deniz. Do not reduce me to only my successes, because then you are taking away my victory, how challenging it was to get to this point."

"I didn't mean it like that." I put a hand on his arm, but he shifted slightly out of my reach. "I was so happy to hear your good news. You deserve those wins, and yes, I was not here to see how hard you worked to get where you are, but my sentiment remains. You are incredible. You have accomplished so much. I am happy for you!"

"Then say the same about yourself," he demanded. "You insist that my glass is half-full, so prove to me that you do not see your own glass as half-empty."

"I — I don't know what you mean." I wasn't in the frame of mind to think highly of myself. A lot in my life needed to change, but I wasn't sure exactly what or where to begin. I had a long way to go.

"You know what I mean," he pressed. "You are empathetic to everyone, except yourself."

He was annoyed, but he still spoke carefully, like when someone who loves you deeply asks a hard question.

"Deniz, why do you think you are not good enough?"

I shrugged, afraid to offer my opinion again. My thoughts remained unchanged.

"Let me explain something to you," Kader began. "I think we're all trying to do our best to figure it out as we go. The tough truth is, the world we were promised when we were growing up is not what was delivered. The life we were supposed to have is not what is available to us now. This messes everything up. Generations of planning, all that labour, years of hard work thrown in to the trash. All that effort people put in, and for what? Where is our reward after all that punishment? We have very little to show for it. Instead, people are desperate, greedy for more of the little things that keep us going — the things that give us a reason to live another week, another six months, another five years. Maybe we are interested in starting a new personal project and seeing where it takes us, or someone invites us on a trip abroad, or a band you like is having a concert soon. Maybe that next relationship will be the one, or a friend will promise us a surprise at our next milestone birthday — all of these events are what give us enough will to keep moving through life. We hang onto them and pretend that it is enough. Some of us can't pretend, though. We refuse to overlook what is owed to us, what we should have received. Ignorance is not a tool that we have in our toolbox. We stubbornly reject the idea that *this* is all there is to life — and then people like us become scary to everyone else."

"What do you mean?" I asked anxiously.

"We threaten the rhythm that society has chosen to follow," Kader elaborated. "We disrupt the peace, demand for people to stay awake rather than drift through life like a daydream, blindly following a pattern that no longer serves us. People like us are terrifying to the system. We threaten its shakedown. So, to protect itself from collapse, society makes us into the enemy. They call us 'depressed,' among other things, in hopes of scaring off the idea that we were right all along. If everyone woke up, society's systems would be under threat, because if enough people were aware of this situation, it could lead to a global revolution. Instead, society turns us into the monster, gives us an incurable illness that threatens to spread, so that others do not give in to that same awareness. Create the idea of depression and then intimidate others into choosing that minimal, basic subscription for life. Society is protecting itself at the cost of humanity."

"You seem very passionate about this subject," I said, a little worried about him.

"Because I know what it is like to sink into the void." There was pain in Kader's voice. "I will never look down on someone who is struggling because I have been there, too, but my point is — many of us are dealing with a problem that is bigger than us. I will never allow you to speak poorly about yourself as you fight something that is already difficult to overcome on a good day — and with an army behind you. Do not underestimate how hard it has been for each of us to make it to this point, including you. You have come so far in your healing and growing. You will get through this part, too, Deniz."

"But Kader, my dear friend, it does not feel that way." I felt like I could be transparent with him. Like the poet Dilek, he was so decided in his opinions that I thought maybe he could help steer me in the right direction.

"I do not feel like I have accomplished anything," I continued. "It's like I have much to do, but no idea what exactly."

"Canım, shall I speak your thoughts aloud for you?" He spoke with more tenderness this time. "I won't call it cheating, because you already know the answer. You're just so lost in your own mind, and in the words that you think you should be saying, that you no longer trust yourself. I'll attempt it for you, but challenge me if my words don't sit right. Okay?"

"Go on then, help me articulate it."

"You see, you keep comparing yourself to others, including me," Kader began, like a parent teaching their child a lesson. "You put me on this pedestal, thinking I'm so far above you. You think I'm somehow stronger, smarter, more accomplished, more deserving, compared to you. You think I'm further along in life and that you've been left behind. That's what you see when you look at the world, right, Deniz? That many are ahead of you and beyond what you can attain for yourself. That's your view, right? No, canım, don't do that. Remember the answer. You already know that is not the way."

"Hmm." I was processing his point. "I am following you so far."

"Deniz, you don't actually see me," he said. "You are looking at where I am, but you do not see it properly. You see what you believe, you see where you *think* I am, but this is only your *perception* of reality. It is not reality. *You* put me on this pedestal, but if you were to ask me how I feel about it, then you would know that I hate it. I detest this spot within your mind, because it's isolating and lonely over here. Don't put me up there, because I am *not* there. Ask me where I am in life, and I'll tell you that I am *absolutely not* on a pedestal looking down at you or anyone else, for that matter. You have to really listen to me and hear my words, Deniz. No one is above you."

I stared at the concrete walkway of the pier, a little ashamed of myself for the way that I spoke to him earlier. Kader was able to see right through me.

"I am not up there, because life doesn't work that way," Kader went on. "I am not above, or ahead, or more worthy in any way, because we do not walk the same path. We are not competing against each other. How can we compete when our routes are not the same? We do not start from the same place either. We are different people. We are our experiences, thoughts, feelings, and goals, and we are influenced by the generations that came before us, composed of people who were each unique in their own way, too. We cannot be compared. It is impossible. Why do you insist on it? We will never be the same, and that is the essence of life — we are all destined to go our own unique ways. How amazing is that?"

"But seeing how much you've accomplished makes me so proud of you," I told him. "It motivates me to try harder, aim higher."

"And that part is okay. I appreciate it, I do," he emphasized. "The problem is when you add more value to my experiences than to your own. I am not better than you. You are not better than me. You can still be happy for me while also protecting your own progress and not diminishing your own successes."

Coexistence. I had not considered it before. Kader was suggesting that I balance my desire for more and my appreciation for what I have. It felt uncomfortable, but in the way that new shoes are difficult to walk in for a whole day. Now that I think about it, wasn't I already practised with this concept? My whole Turkish-Canadian identity is one big study in coexistence, and I have learned to harmonize those two halves of me well. His idea didn't seem so intimidating anymore.

"I think I understand the difference a bit more now," I said truthfully.

"We can check in on each other, provide support and encouragement for each other's journey. That is community and partnership. We must give everyone the chance for the same opportunities to ensure that no one person's journey is rigged against them. This is human rights. We look within ourselves for our strengths and take guidance from the energies around us — that is spirituality."

"Kader, you have become very wise." I looked at him more closely. "I wonder what kind of hardship you've endured to give way for this awakening. You really do use that philosophy degree." He ignored me and pulled down on his sleeves, likely cold from the Bosphorus's evening breeze.

"I will say it again," Kader started. "We will never walk the same path, and this is how life goes. I am not trying to be so hard on you. I tell you this out of my respect and care for you. You and I are not the same. I am so honoured to know you, Deniz. I applaud your willingness to learn and to keep going through the trials that life gives you. I try to do the same. I am grateful that you think well of me as I navigate my own way. More than anything, I hope your path takes you somewhere wonderful. That one, by the way, is called love."

"And how is the path I'm on then?" I asked softly. "How can I know if I'm headed somewhere beautiful?"

"Only you have that knowledge." Kader put a firm hand on my shoulder. We stood and he guided me along the edge of the waterfront.

"Our paths are created as we walk them," he said as we embarked on a nighttime stroll. "Some of it is predestined, but much is in your control. It depends on your choices and how you react to the world. I can offer encouragement, but not much more. All I can say for now is to try and make your story a good one."

I let his advice settle into a comfortable place in my mind. His words were familiar.

"You are still reassuring and good-natured, just like when we were children," I said with a sigh. "Where have you been?"

"That part of me hasn't changed, but my road was not always so warm and fuzzy." The corners of his mouth turned slightly downwards. "Like many others, of course, I have suffered. I am not so special. I also suspect that life is not yet finished feeding me its sourness."

His words grew quieter. My old friend must have seen the worry return to my face, because he squeezed my shoulder a little tighter then.

"Merak etme, Deniz" he assured me, but only his mouth was smiling. "I've had my fair share of low days, and they were torture. My situation was serious, I admit. I was coping. I'm glad you didn't witness that part." He took in a short breath before continuing. "Some days, I did not want to live to see another, and I didn't care who would miss me. I can share that with you now, but I couldn't say it aloud back then."

He glanced at me for a second and decided to go on. "Within that purgatory of my mind, so to speak, I weighed the reasons for choosing life over death. To tell you the truth, I was surprised at the answers that swam to the surface when

I gave myself a chance to really think about it. I'll skip the details, but I focused on trying to find a way forward and led with curiosity. Honestly, Deniz, as the days passed, I thankfully found more reasons to wake up every day, but even now, I have to actively choose life. That decision does not yet come naturally to me, but at least now I can say that I am truly living. Each day is a gift that I give to myself. And look, I have had the good fortune of walking beside you again." The smile returned to his eyes. It pierced me.

Kader spoke with authority but also with a softness that I had never found in someone else. He looked a little tired, but his spirit felt powerful, as if the world didn't scare him anymore. Though his confession couldn't be taken lightly, I wasn't worried about him. He had adapted, evolved. He found his way out of that mess, and I couldn't help but feel more hopeful for myself as a result.

"Tell me," I said. "I want to hear what has happened on this path of yours. Give me the chance to encourage you, too."

"We'll take turns," he said, laughing. "You take a lokum, then I'll take one. Back and forth we'll go, tasting all the flavours until the bowl is empty."

"Haydi," I agreed. "I've got some time."

• • •

There were no splashing waves now, just steady water along the pier. My feet sizzled as the day's exhaustion caught up to me. I felt every step of my day spent wandering İstanbul in the ache in my calves. The long day nestled into my mid-back. The heat of the sun warmed my skin still, despite its absence, and I could just make out the tan I'd managed to acquire. The tightness within my chest was detangling, my mind clearing.

In the depths of my stomach, I still savoured the stories that this day had fed my soul, but I was not yet satisfied. I knew there were more out there, and certainly, I had a few tales of my own to share. These people that I'd met as I wandered İstanbul, they might not know how much they'd helped me, but they had, each and every one of them. Their anecdotes had provided insights into their lives, their lessons, their treasures. Not just the people but also the land and the buildings that I explored today — they spoke to me, too.

Seeking the next story is a good way forward, I believe. Yes, let's try it, now that I can attest to how helpful a good tale can be. I might try to write my own narrative. I think I want to make it small but flavourful. I want it to be carried around, exchanging hands and storytellers. I'm tired of heavy conclusions; I want my story to dissolve into a sweet ending. Like a bedtime story or a folk tale that can be told over and over again, with each retelling having the potential to draw the listener's attention to something new. It could live at the border between dream and existence. Its promise for adventure will coat the palate. Its aftertaste will be memorable. A story only for people who need to digest it but who still want a delightful treat to act as their medicine.

I don't know what direction the narrative will take, but I know it must start with me and maybe those famous opening lines, "Bir varmış, bir yokmuş." I haven't planned that far ahead yet. I think that I will just start to tell it and see where it goes. I can always change the narrative as I go along, switch up my rug's design.

Finally, and maybe most importantly, I need someone to hear it. A story can only be breathed to life once it is told to another's listening ear. It will not survive in the mind, because the mind is all-consuming. No, that will not do. I need someone who loves stories, because only that sort of person will know how to receive mine. I need an active participant, someone who understands and agrees to this mission. A person to assist me in keeping this story alive. Who could I approach with this request? Oh yes, of course, I just thought of someone.

Yolcu yolunda gerek.

[illegible]

I don't know what direction the narrative will take. I just know it must start with me and my [illegible] lines [illegible] but [illegible] ahead [illegible] that I will just start [illegible] and see where it [illegible]. I can always change the narrative as I go along with [illegible] design.

Finally, and maybe most importantly, I need someone to narrate. A story can only be created in [illegible] someone [illegible] someone who [illegible] stories [illegible] will know how to [illegible] someone who [illegible] and [illegible] to the [illegible]. [illegible] And [illegible] What would I [illegible] of course [illegible] someone.

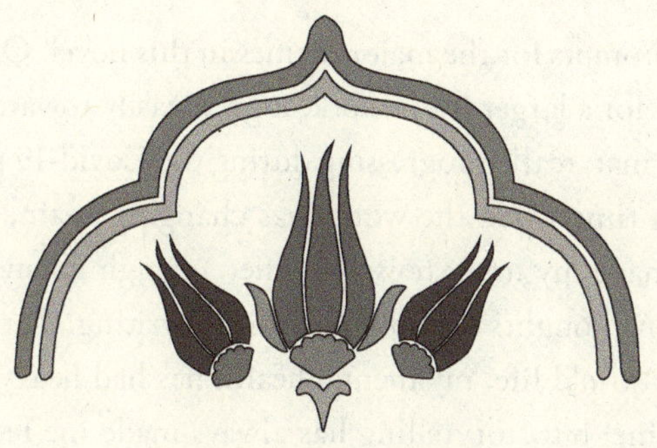

AUTHOR'S NOTE

This work is a reflection of my own experiences in the opening thirty years of my life, compiled into a narrated travelling adventure and told over the course of one fictional day. My hope is that readers will take this book with them and retrace my steps around İstanbul to freshen up their perspectives on life or to be inspired to recreate the process in their own cities. Especially in the modern world, I feel the need to express how the pursuit of happiness always seems to be fleeting, and yet we see it more clearly by the day. As someone who embraces two cultures and two perspectives on life, I aim to help readers see how I live in this world and to acknowledge those with similar experiences and help them feel understood.

I began writing this book more than a decade ago, simply because I love creative writing and sharing my culture with others. I would take out a notebook to randomly jot down notes whenever a phrase came to me, and these would later act as prompts for the major themes in this novel. Once I got an idea for a larger framework, it grew easily toward its current format, really progressing during the Covid-19 pandemic. At a time when the world was changing again, its outer noise made my inner noise go quiet, enough for me to hear my own thoughts and put them into writing. Throughout my not-so-old life, my mental health has had heavy pockets of decline, but storytelling has always made me feel better. Whether having a simple catch-up conversation over coffee, mentoring others, watching an insightful TV series, reading a book that was recommended to me, or writing poetry, I am my best self when there is a story to be shared. Not just when I was feeling inspired, but more often on my hardest days, I would write passages of this book, and my mood would improve. Even after the book was finished and ready for editing, in September 2024, I would reread sections of it on days when those flowers in the garden were drowned by shadows. My hope is that readers will return to this novel throughout their lives and find comfort and familiarity in a different chapter each time.

I found that my efforts for protecting my mental health — practising mindfulness and discussing hard thoughts with trusted peers — all played a key role in asking those spiritual questions without fear or judgment. An exercise for the soul. I certainly do not pretend to be a therapist, but I've become rather familiar with my own inner world. More specifically,

I wanted to stress the importance of storytelling and of depending on your community: to uplift you, to provide you with clarity and direction, and to share your community's learnings via its members' own stories. If anything, I wish for this book to inspire the exchange of stories, to awaken us again, to help us feel safer within this world, and to bring us closer together.

All the characters in this novel are fictional; however, this story is inspired by my own experiences, my family and friends, acquaintances that I never liked, even a random foreigner who dared to share their story with me during their travels. Each side character that the protagonist comes across offers their own teachings, like a new kind of lokum to taste on our journey through İstanbul. I have many more stories and thoughts to share, but for this book, I picked my favourite flavours. My goal was to keep this novel the size of a pocketbook to take with you on your travels — a light read but without superficial content. The novel is also written with a cyclical form, where the reader can bridge the last chapter and the first chapter, as if listening to a story on a loop.

I had a few inspirations for how I wanted to write this novel, particularly in relation to the style of books that I myself enjoy reading. I grew up loving the embedded storytelling mechanics of *Arabian Nights* and the charm of short stories. I was entertained by the human existential crisis that comes up in *The Stranger*, by French novelist Albert Camus, who takes on the dilemma by giving his main character a kind of nonchalant attitude on the subject. Books by author Khaled Hosseini, such as *The Kite Runner* and *A Thousand Splendid Suns*, introduce readers to cultural expressions in an authentic and unapologetic writing style. There are other books that I love, which follow the same aesthetics as the ones mentioned above, and I hope you find these books already overtaking your bookshelves.

It was important to me that I was able to share Turkish words and phrases with the readers, but in the way that I define them. The interconnectedness of my languages is how I primarily think and see the world, so I could not imagine writing this narrative any differently. There are no encyclopedic definitions in this novel, only my own interpretations, considering how I grew up in between languages, so I hope readers are forgiving of my definitions in the glossary. Another detail that I insisted on incorporating was the selection of character names. In Turkish culture, like in many others, name meanings hold significance and are often comparable with a person's personality. Throughout this book, character names were carefully chosen to reflect subthemes of the book and to emphasize character traits. Different cultures and languages might have variances on the meanings below, but here are my definitions of the character names selected for this novel (in order of their appearance):

Asaf — collector, gatherer; virtue; vizier
Nergiz — daffodil; rebirth and new beginnings
Timur — man of iron
Karga — crow
Ateş — fire
Yağmur — rain; living; prosperous
Osman — youthful; wise and intuitive; powerful
Ece — queen
Emre — friend; passionate
Renard — fox, cunning; a strong decision
Serap — mirage, imagination; fanciful
Ömer — to live long, prospering
Hakan — supreme ruler, great king, emperor
Dilek — wish, desire, request
Deren — gatherer of flowers
Defne — laurel
Ela — hazel
Aydın — enlightened
Göçmenoğlu — son/child of an immigrant
Özgür — independent
Semiha — the one who forgives
Efe — older brother
Deniz — sea
Kader — fate; destiny

• • •

Some characters do not have names, and that is intended to make them more approachable. I hoped that the reader would feel more connected to the character without my imposing an identity onto them. Similarly, I especially wanted the main character to remain anonymous for as long as possible, and for their name to be gender-neutral, as a way to invite readers to find parts of themselves within the protagonist. The Turkish language is also gender-neutral, which plays well with my intent. I eliminated reasons for Deniz to stand out as someone with unique features and allowed them to be more of a mirror for readers — to see themselves reflected in this story.

While I still have your attention, I want to acknowledge the invaluable people who have supported me in this process and speak directly to them with the reader as my witness: A warm and expanding thank-you to the team at Dundurn Press who worked diligently on this book. You have all treated my first novel with great care. To Andrea, my editor, who read my heart on every page, you have been very considerate in your edits to my work. I am truly thankful.

Thank you to the dearest friends who have joined me for writing sessions with a cup of coffee and the comfort of your company. I felt very much at ease thanks to your presence and your reassurance for me to write. I wrote these chapters so freely thanks to each of you. You allowed me to speak the same feelings repeatedly until they finally made sense to me, and I cannot be more grateful. Thank you to the ones who recommended books for me to read, knowing that more stories would feed my ever-hungry mind. I will not forget it and feel very fortunate for my path to have crossed with yours. I wish to thank my parents, who were often eager to read a chapter before I finished it and who encouraged me to run away to those cafés to write them faster. I want to thank my Abla (older sister), to whom this book is dedicated, for being my very first reader a long time ago and who is just as enthusiastic as me to hear a good story. I thank you for holding a special place in your overflowing bookshelf for my novel. This chosen family has saved me many times through their own storytelling, so I am sending my sincerest expressions of appreciation for all of you. You can imagine me giving you a really long hug.

Finally, like a piece of Turkish delight at the end of bitter coffee, a small but powerfully sweet message of thanks to you. Thank you to the readers and fellow storytellers who gave my first novel a chance to shine. May you receive the same grace and respect when your story is told.

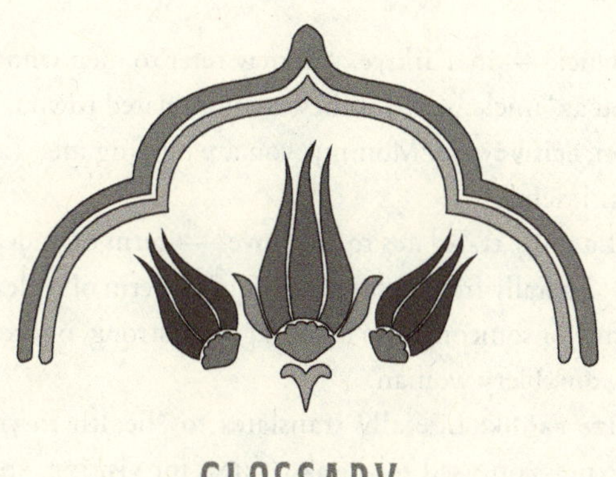

GLOSSARY

TURKISH WORDS AND EXPRESSIONS

Abi: Older brother — in Türkiye, you may refer to a man who is only slightly older than you as "older brother," even if they are not related to you.

Aferin: Well done.

Agh: Turkish expression — a sound that Turkish people make to express being in pain. It can be used for literal physical pain, to mean disappointment, or used sarcastically to show deep satisfaction (as in this case).

ajda: Turkish tea glass in an hourglass shape, nicknamed after famous singer Ajda Pekkan.

akıllı çocuğum benim: My smart child.

allah akıl dağıtırken, sen kapının arkasında mı kaldın: When God was handing out intelligence, were you left behind the door?

Allahallah: An expression implying that something is ridiculous or unbelievable.

Amca: Uncle — in Türkiye, you may refer to men who are older than you as "uncle," even if they are not related to you.

Annecim, acıtıyorsun: Mommy, you are hurting me.

arkadaş: Friend.

aşkım: Literally translates to "my love" — term of endearment.

aslanım: Literally translates to "my lion" — term of endearment; a nickname for someone who is courageous, strong, or exceptional.

ateşli kadın: Fiery woman.

Ayağınıza sağlık: Literally translates to "health to your feet" — an expression used to thank a guest for visiting, specifically thanking the guest's feet for carrying them to you.

Ayaklarını sürttün: Literally translates to "You wiped your feet (on the doormat)" — a Turkish expression meaning that a single customer has brought more business to a store by just being there, symbolizing that they created good luck and fortune for the business.

Ayasofya: Hagia Sophia Mosque (Ayasofya Camii)

azan: Call to prayer.

balık ekmek: Fish bread — street food made by quickly frying small and oily fish (like mackerel), and placing it in white baguette-style bread, with an assortment of sautéed vegetables and condiments.

balım: Literally translates to "my honey" — term of endearment.

Başınız sağolsun: My condolences/Sorry for your loss.

Bay: Sir/mister.

bayram: Holiday.

Bekle: Wait.

Bir kişilik, lütfen: Table for one, please.

Bir varmış, bir yokmuş: Literally translates to "Once there was, once there wasn't…" — the equivalent to "Once upon a time."

There is an extended fairytale introduction in Turkish, but this line is the shortened version.

Boş ver: Forget it/leave it.

Buyrun: Welcome/Can I help you?

canım: Literally translates to "my life" — term of endearment. The English equivalent is hard to capture, because the true meaning is deeper than "life" and closer in meaning to the source of one's life.

canım arkadaşım: My dearest friend.

çaycı: Tea maker/server.

[name]cim or [name]cım: In Turkish, adding "cim" or "cım" (pronounced *jim* or *jeum* depending on the name) to the end of a person's name adds familiarity and playfulness. In other Middle Eastern languages, the suffix is pronounced *jahn* or *joon*, and carries the same sense of endearment.

çoban: Literally translates to "shepherd," but in this case refers to a salad made with finely chopped staple garden produce, including tomatoes, cucumber, and onion, with olive oil and lemon juice.

çocuğum: My child.

çocuklar: Children.

derbi: Derby — in the Turkish soccer league, this is a domestic match played between two high-tier teams that are characteristically defined as rivals.

Dikkat: Careful.

dönerci: A shawarma place.

Ellerinize sağlık: Literally translates to "Health to your hands" — an expression used to thank someone for high-quality work done with their hands, such as cooking or crafting.

emekli çay: Literally translates to "retired tea" — this nickname gives the impression that retired Turkish people don't usually make strong tea because they have no need to anymore. Sometimes called açık çay (light tea), this is a weaker Turkish tea, where there is a higher water ratio to make the tea less concentrated.

En kısa zamanda görüşmek üzere: Literally translates to "Until we meet again and in the shortest amount of time possible" — an informal and friendly way to sign off a letter or end a conversation.

erik: A type of plum, which can be eaten ripe (purple and sweet) or underripe (green and sour). There is also a less common plum that is mild and yellowish white.

eski türkü: Turkish folk songs and music with traditional instruments.

fal: Fortune-telling — in this case, it is referring to Turkish coffee fortunes.

fıstık: Literally translates to "peanut" — an affectionate nickname for a beautiful woman.

Gel: Come here/over.

Gençler buyursun: Youth are welcome.

Görüşürüz: We'll see each other soon.

Gözünü seveyim: Literally translates to "Let me love your eye/perspective" — this Turkish expression is said with a tone of annoyance and usually indicates being exasperated with someone. It means "I beg of you" or "For goodness' sake."

Güle güle: Literally translates to "Go laughing/smiling" — an expression to wish someone well when they leave you.

Halıcılar Caddesi: Street of rug makers/sellers.

hanımeli: Honeysuckle flower.

hayatım: Literally translates to "my life" — term of endearment, closer in meaning to "my everything," used to express that the person represents everything that is important to you.
Haydi: "Come on" or "Let's go." The correct spelling is "Hadi," but "Haydi" is usually pronounced with playfulness and enthusiasm.
Ha gayret: Literally translates to "Come on, put in the effort" or "You can endure/overcome it" — an expression that offers encouragement to complete a task.
hocam: Literally translates to "my professor" ("hoca" by itself means "professor," "teacher," "scholar," etc.). In Turkish, strangers from the older generation are addressed as "my teacher" to emphasize respect for their extensive life experience. Of course, actual professors who teach higher education can also be called "hoca," and imams are sometimes called "hoca" as well.
Hoş geldiniz: Welcome.
İstiklal Cadde: Independence Street.
itiraflar: Confessions.
İznik: A town in the Bursa province, best known for its signature pottery and tile design. Thus, İznik also refers to a particular style of painted ceramic.
Kapalı Çarşı: Literally translates to "the covered market" — it is known in English as the Grand Bazaar.
kardeşim: Younger sibling — in Türkiye, you may refer to any person who is slightly younger than you as "younger sibling," even if they are not related to you.
Kesenize bereket: An expression of gratitude after someone has paid for you, wishing that Allah grants that person even more wealth so that their generosity is reciprocated.
kocam: My husband.

köfte: A flat, spiced, Middle Eastern meatball.

Kolay gelsin: May your work come easy to you.

kolonya: A multi-purpose alcoholic solution that usually smells of lemon, though other scents are available. It is typically used as a hand sanitizer but is also good for cleaning cuts and removing stains and can be used as aftershave and to soothe upset stomachs with just its scent. It is a Turkish person's remedy for everything.

Korkma, şekerim: Don't be afraid, my sweet.

kumpir: Type of Turkish street food — a large baked potato with various toppings and sauces.

kuzum: My lamb.

lahmacun: A type of very thin dough that is lightly charred in a stone oven. It is topped with pressed and spiced ground beef mixed with tomato and herbs. Once cooked, the bread is usually filled with freshly sliced tomatoes, parsley, and onions and is rolled before eating. It is a cheap food that most closely resembles a very thin pizza covered with toppings and rolled like a burrito.

limonata: Turkish lemonade, often sweeter and more intensely flavoured than North American lemonade. It is usually served very cold, either with ice or as a slushy.

lokum: Turkish delight — a small, chewy candy.

Maşallah: Literally translates to "Allah has willed it" — an expression of praise or to acknowledge greatness.

maydonoz: Literally translates to "parsley" — term for directing insult; this nickname is given to someone who is being annoying, like parsley getting stuck in one's teeth.

mayıştım: A slang verb (infinitive, slang: mayışmak) expressing the feeling of being warm and sleepy — wanting rest after lots of eating, drinking, exercising, and/or staying out in the sun. Possibly connected to the word "maya" (yeast), which also requires moisture, heat, nutrients, and rest.

Merak etme: Do not worry — the root meaning of this expression is closer to "Do not be curious/anxious/wonder."

mola: Taking a break — used to express an intermission or stopover.

Müşteri var: A customer is here.

nazar boncuk: An evil eye bead — typically a blue-and-white glass bead — meant to ward off negative energy (nazar) from others. A very common pendant or amulet in cultures originating primarily in the Fertile Crescent region.

Ne?: What?

nektarin: Nectarine.

orta: Medium — for Turkish coffee, this order adds a very small amount of sugar into the coffee.

pazar: Weekly outdoor market.

pide: Turkish pizza, typically diamond-shaped.

rahatsız eder: To make one feel disturbed or uncomfortable.

Ramazan: Ramadan.

Rica ederim: No problem at all/My pleasure.

Ruhuna Fatiha: A phrase referring to the opening chapters of the Quran. It literally means "Fatiha for their soul," and is the start of the Sura al-Fatiha prayer. An equivalent expression on a tombstone is "Rest in peace." The "D" in Turkish stands for doğum tarihi (birth date), and the "Ö" stands for ölüm tarihi (death date).

sade: Plain — this Turkish coffee order has no sugar, making it very strong and bitter.

şerbetci: A traditionally dressed juice seller.

simit: Like a sesame bagel, but one that is dipped in tahini to create a hard outer shell, coated in baked sesame seeds.

Su akar, yolu bulur: Literally translates to "Water flows/drips [and] finds a way" — a Turkish proverb that means you will overcome obstacles naturally; it is only a matter of time. No additional stress or effort is required for your perseverance; fate has taken care of your plans. Your success is already within you.

Sultanahmet Meydanı: Sultanahmet Square is a park sandwiched between two historic buildings: the Blue Mosque (Sultan Ahmet Camii) and Hagia Sophia Mosque (Ayasofya Camii).

Tamam: Okay.

Tanıdığınız mı?: Is it someone you know?

tatlı kızım: My sweet daughter.

tatlım: Literally translates to "my sweet" — term of endearment.

Tebrik ederim: Congratulations.

terbiyesizler: People who live without manners.

Teyze: Aunt — in Türkiye, you may refer to women who are older than you as "aunt," even if they are not related to you.

Türküm: I'm Turkish.

Usta: Literally translates to "Master" — a nickname given to an expert, or someone who has mastered their craft.

Vay: An expression of surprise — or the Turkish sound for being impressed. Equivalent to "Wow!"

vişne: Sour cherry.

yavrum: My cub.

Yazıklar olsun: Shame on you.

Yerebatan Sarnıcı: Basilica Cistern, another historical landmark in İstanbul. It is an ancient Roman underground water reserve covering almost ten thousand square metres and has served as a temporary art space in recent years.

Yok yok: No way.

yolcu: Traveller or passenger — this term is used for both domestic and foreign individuals.

Yolcu yolunda gerek: Travellers must return to their travel/road — an expression that means you have a long journey ahead, so you need to get going. This phrase is usually said when someone has finished taking a break or has finished visiting another person. It can be directed at yourself or to the person that you are with at the time.

Yolunuz açık olsun: May your road/journey be open/go smoothly.

Zamanı geldi: Literally translates to "The moment has come" — can be used in the literal sense, but is also an expression Turkish people sometimes use to end a conversation before leaving.

Zincirli Han: Literally translates to "caravanserai of chains" — meaning a procession of goods laid out for sale, it is also called the Jeweller's Gate.

TURKISH GESTURES

In order of appearance within the novel.

Taking a person's right hand and raising it to touch your chin and forehead: In Türkiye, elders are greeted or thanked by taking their right hand, giving it a "kiss" by touching the back of it to your chin, and then lifting it to touch your forehead. It is one of the highest signs of respect and is a way to greet or say goodbye to an elder.

Quick head tilt down: A quick nod down is an affirmation and an acknowledgement. It is the same as saying, "Yes" or "Of course" or "Much appreciated." Sometimes the motion is accompanied by a long blink; however, a nod upward that is matched with raised eyebrows and a *tsk* of the tongue is the same as saying no in an informal way.

Palm tap to the chest: A full hand performing two quick taps to the chest (or sometimes one tap) indicates a respectful rejection. It is roughly equivalent to saying, "I'm all good" or "I've had my fill."

ABOUT THE AUTHOR

Photo by Duane Cole

SELİN KAHRAMANOĞLU is a Turkish-Canadian museum and archives professional, researcher, artist, writer, and educator. In 2020, she graduated from the University of Toronto with a master of museum studies and a master of information with a concentration in archives and records management. A recipient of the Ontario Museum Association's Excellence in Emerging Museum Practice Award, she has worked with several cultural institutions internationally and partnered with Turkish organizations to support the development of Near and Middle Eastern community-building in Canada. Her curatorial work focuses on material culture interpretation through art, history, literature, food, ceremony, and land. She explores themes of meaning-making in intersectionality, highlighting invisible minorities, exploring intergenerational mentorship, and expressions of mental health. Selin has taught cultural courses and facilitated workshops for all ages, particularly youth and young professionals. *Lokum* is her first novel. She currently lives in Ontario, though you will often find her at a café in İstanbul.